"This is a police matter."

He raced from the room, his mind looping with Lacey's first three words—"I was attacked"—and realized with some surprise that he wanted to hurt the person who'd hurt her.

Forty-five seconds later, when he saw her sitting against the side of the building with an ice pack on her cheek, the rage inside him tripled and he knew without a doubt that past or no past, betrayal or no betrayal, he was going to fall for Lacey Gibson once again.

And wondered how he was going to keep his heart from being ripped in two when it happened.

Books by Lynette Eason

Love Inspired Suspense

Lethal Deception
River of Secrets
Holiday Illusion
A Silent Terror
A Silent Fury
A Silent Pursuit
My Deadly Valentine
   "Dark Obsession"
Protective Custody
Missing

LYNETTE EASON

grew up in Greenville, SC. Her home church, Northgate Baptist, had a tremendous influence on her during her early years. She credits Christian parents and dedicated Sunday school teachers for her acceptance of Christ at the tender age of eight. Even as a young girl, she knew she wanted her life to reflect the love of Jesus.

Lynette attended the University of South Carolina in Columbia, SC, then moved to Spartanburg, SC, to attend Converse College, where she obtained her master's degree in education. During that time, she met the boy next door, Jack Eason, and married him. Jack is the executive director of the Sound of Light Ministries. Lynette and Jack have two precious children—Lauryn, eight years old, and Will, who is six. She and Jack are members of New Life Baptist Fellowship Church in Boiling Springs, SC, where Jack serves as the worship leader and Lynette teaches Sunday school to the four- and five-year-olds.

Missing

LYNETTE EASON

Steeple
Hill®

Published by Steeple Hill Books™

STEEPLE HILL BOOKS

Steeple
Hill®

Recycling programs
for this product may
not exist in your area.

ISBN-13: 978-0-373-67447-3

MISSING

www.SteepleHill.com

Printed in U.S.A.

"My son" the father said, "you are always with me, and everything I have is yours. But we had to celebrate and be glad, because this brother of yours was dead and is alive again; he was lost and is found."

—*Luke* 15:31–32

To my family. I love you all!

ONE

"My daughter's missing and I need your help."

Mason stared down at the distraught redheaded woman standing on his front porch, tears swimming in her eyes, fists clenched at her side.

Shock immobilized him for a brief moment, then with an effort, he found his voice.

"Lacey Gibson." Just saying her name transported him to the past. His first love. His first romantic heartbreak. She hadn't changed a bit.

At least on the outside.

If her heart was as traitorous as he remembered, he was in deep trouble.

The fact that his own heart did its best to leap from his chest in joyous welcome surprised him so much he almost swallowed his tongue.

What was she doing here? And what had she said? His brain had ceased to function the minute he realized who'd knocked on his door.

Stepping toward him, she placed her hands on his chest, tears threatening to spill from those green eyes that had captivated him at first glance. She pleaded, "I need your help. Bethany's missing and no one seems to know why, or who she may have disappeared with—and no one seems to even care or want to listen to what I have to say or—"

A finger over her lips effectively cut off her monologue—and sent fire shooting along his nerve endings. He remembered covering those sweet lips with his, kissing her until they were both breathless and...

First things first. "What are you doing here and who is Bethany?"

She seemed oblivious to the fact that she still had her hands on his chest. He wasn't in any hurry for her to remove them.

Much to his disgust.

Was he still so besotted with her that he'd forgotten what she'd done to him sixteen years ago?

No way. He'd gotten over her a long time ago.

Or so he tried to convince himself.

And yet somehow he found himself standing in his foyer with Lacey Gibson practically wrapped in his arms—and liking it.

Clearing his throat, he stepped back, took her hand—a soft hand, he noted—and pulled her into the den. There, he deposited her on the couch and asked, "Do you need a drink of water?

Some coffee?" He looked at the tears that had now spilled over to track their way down her pale cheeks. "A tissue?"

"Yes to the tissue, no to the drink."

Mason reached around her and, with only a twinge of pain in his left shoulder, snatched a tissue from the end table and handed it to her. The only reason Lacey had found him at home at ten-thirty on a Tuesday morning was because he'd been forbidden to go back to work for another two weeks.

Being shot in the line of duty had been a real pain. Both physically and mentally. As a Deputy U.S. Marshal, he was used to action and staying busy. Being out on medical leave was definitely not on his top-one-hundred-favorite-things-to-do list. But he was almost finished with that.

And he had a feeling his days of boredom had just come to an end. She had a daughter? His gut tightened. "Why do you think she's missing, and what do you think I can do to find her?" What he wanted to ask was why she'd chosen to come to him about it. Instead, he leaned back against the couch and studied the woman before him.

Her fiery red curls were pulled up into some kind of scrunchy thing women seemed to like. Her normally sparkling green eyes were set in an oval-shaped face that looked pale and drawn, stressed and tired. Light gray bags under her eyes attested to some lost sleep.

But she was still beautiful, and his heart warmed.

Which meant she could still be dangerous, his head argued.

His heart agreed, but from the way it threatened to beat out of his chest, Mason didn't think it cared.

She raised the tissue and swiped a few tears then took a deep breath. "Bethany is my fifteen-year-old daughter. She's been gone for two days now." She looked at the ceiling. "Today's Tuesday. I last saw her Sunday morning when I went to wake her up for church. She mumbled that she didn't feel good so I let her sleep. When I got home, she wasn't there. I called her cell phone and she didn't answer."

"Does she usually answer when you call?"

Lacey blinked and took another swipe at the tears. "Yes, usually. So, I waited awhile, then tried again. And kept trying. When I *still* didn't hear anything, I called a few of her friends. The ones that I managed to get on the line didn't know where she was. When she wasn't home and hadn't called by dark, I went looking for her. I couldn't find her, so I started calling all of her friends again. Not one of them knew…" Her breath hitched and more tears leaked. She turned wet emerald-green eyes on him, pleading. "She's not answering her cell phone and she missed school yesterday...." She lifted her hands and swallowed. "I went to the police and they're treating her as a runaway. No one else will do anything and I just don't know what else to do. Please help me, Mason."

Lacey bit her lip and stared up at the man as if he were her last hope. He still wore his reddish-blond hair in a military buzz cut. A hysterical laugh bubbled in her throat. Why had she even noticed that?

Focusing on his startling blue eyes, the same eyes she'd looked into every day for the past fifteen years, she decided that while she hated to come begging for his help, she'd do it for Bethany.

Where Bethany was concerned, the only thing that mattered was finding her. And if working with the man who'd broken her heart sixteen years ago meant she could bring her daughter home safely, she'd do it without a second thought.

What she hadn't told Mason was that it wasn't just Bethany that she needed help with. Since her daughter's disappearance, she had felt watched. Like eyes followed her wherever she went. It was creepy and unsettling.

But nothing else had happened. So she'd started to wonder if it was all her imagination.

Bethany's disappearance confirmed it wasn't.

Even as she walked up the steps to Mason's front porch, she had to resist looking back over her shoulder. She shuddered.

And just last night, she'd paced the house, praying, calling out to God and thought she heard someone at the door. Thinking it was Bethany, she'd flung it open and found a page from her old high school yearbook tacked to her door.

Confused, she'd pulled it down and stared out into the night. The hair on the nape of her neck had prickled, and a sense of foreboding had nearly overcome her.

One thing she knew for sure: someone was watching her. But who? Bethany's possible kidnapper?

"Give me back my daughter!" she'd screamed. "Where is she?"

No one had answered.

But she'd felt the lingering eyes on her, watching from beyond, the malice, the—evil? Gulping, she'd shut the door and leaned against it, a hand to her throat. What was she going to do?

The answer had come to her—and not one she'd liked. She knew without a doubt that she had to go to Mason Stone. A man she'd vowed never to see again.

The man who'd broken her heart sixteen years ago.

Now looking into Mason's expressionless face,

she realized she might have made a mistake. She was surprised he'd let her in the door. How she found herself on his couch was anyone's guess. But that didn't matter. Her main focus was Bethany. She had to save her child.

No matter what their past contained. They'd simply have to deal with that later.

Mason stood, shoved his hands into the back pockets of his jeans and paced to the other end of the room, then back. "Why should I help you, Lacey?"

The question, while asked in a voice so low she had to strain to hear it, seemed to echo off the walls of the house and ricochet inside her brain.

"Because…because…"

"Because of our past? Just because we once meant something to each other doesn't mean anything. When you decided to cheat on me with my best friend, you made it clear what you thought of our relationship."

Shock bolted Lacey to her feet. "How dare you? *How dare you?* I never cheated on you! But just like now, you wouldn't stop throwing around accusations long enough to listen!" She snatched another tissue from the box and headed for the door. "Well, I'm not the scared, intimidated little girl I was at eighteen years old. So, never mind. I was wrong. I can't believe how wrong I was."

"I saw you—Daniel said…" Mason sucked in

a deep breath and turned away from her as she stomped for the exit. His low "Stop. Don't go yet" froze her in her tracks.

Without facing him, she asked, "Why shouldn't I?"

"Because you came to me for a reason," he said, then sighed. "It seems the past isn't as dead as I thought it was. I didn't mean to…"

Keeping her voice frigid, she muttered, "Never mind. It doesn't matter. All that matters is finding Bethany. Will you help me or not?"

Fingers wrapped around her upper arm and he swung her around to face him. "I don't know yet. Sit back down. Please. Tell me about Bethany and why you think I can help you."

Clamping down on the desire to hurtle her own accusations, she seated herself on the couch once more and took a deep breath. *For Bethany, remember? You can do this for Bethany.*

So, how much should she tell him?

All of it.

"I thought you could help me because being a marshal…isn't that what you do for a living? Find people?"

He nodded. "Fugitives mostly."

"But you have connections, you can—" She stopped, closed her eyes and sucked in a calming breath. She needed to keep her cool. "Bethany is a good kid." Should she show him the picture?

No, as soon as she did, he would know…. "She's had an emotional and rocky couple of years as all teens do, but things had been getting better since we moved back here."

He nodded, listening.

"Bethany wouldn't just disappear like this. Not at this point in our lives. Not at all." Her daughter might do a lot of things, but running away from home was definitely not one of them. "And not when I've just promised…" She bit her lip and looked away.

"Promised what?"

She straightened her shoulders. "Since I've promised to let her meet her father."

His lips tightened and suspicion narrowed his eyes. "And who is her father?"

"He's…" She sucked in a deep breath. She couldn't just blurt it out. "I'll get to that in a minute." *Oh Lord, I need your help and guidance on this. Right now, please.*

Twisting the tissue between her fingers, she drew in another breath and looked him in the eye. "Some strange things have been happening lately. To Bethany. And I think they're related to the car wreck that happened a couple of months ago."

"What wreck?"

"It was during spring break back in April. Bethany's best friend, Kayla Mahoney, was driving and she ran off the road, hit a tree and—" she pressed shaking fingers to her lips "—died."

Mason's sharply indrawn breath stabilized her. "Wait a minute, I think I heard about that."

Lacey swiped a tear away. "Anyway, after the accident, Bethany was having trouble dealing with it. So, I looked into getting her some help. She started counseling with our pastor and seemed to be improving. And now this." Through clenched teeth she gritted, "But no one seems to be interested in helping me!"

She fought the wave of tears as she looked at Mason.

He rubbed a hand over his face then caught her eye. "And you said weird things started happening after the wreck?"

"Yes."

"Like what?"

"Bethany started acting very strange. She jumped at the slightest noise, refused to go out by herself, became my shadow if we went out together. It seemed she was constantly watching her back, but she adamantly refused to talk about it. She started losing weight, having nightmares. I thought she might be suffering from depression after everything that happened."

"It would certainly be understandable."

Lacey nodded. "Then someone tried to break into our house one night. Bethany came screaming into my room in the middle of the night that someone was climbing in her window. I called the police and they came out, but found nothing that indicated someone tried to get in. But there are bushes and mulch and—" She waved a hand. "It would be impossible to say if there was or wasn't someone out there. The police blamed it on youthful pranks." She rolled her eyes and shook her head.

"What else?" he probed.

"About a week later, she said she thought someone had followed her home from school. We live near the high school, so she walks to and from school. Only in the last few weeks I've had to start taking her and picking her up. She's gotten so frightened that she's refused to go to school unless I drive her."

Mason started pacing again. "Did you report it?"

"Yes."

He frowned. "And that's it?"

Exasperated, Lacey stood and paced to the fireplace then back to her seat. "Yes—and no."

"Meaning?"

"Meaning I think there's more to it."

"Such as?"

"I don't know!" Lacey threw her hands up in frustration. "But I think there was someone else with Kayla that night. I think her friend Georgia

Boyles and—" she swallowed hard "—Bethany were in that car that night."

Mason's brows shot up. "Why do you say that?"

"Because Georgia's mother came to my house to ask Bethany if Georgia had been with Kayla that night."

"Why did she suspect that?"

"Because Georgia came home around three in morning, scratched up and with bruises she couldn't explain. The police also found her cell phone in the car. When they returned it to her she said she'd left it in there earlier that day."

"Could be." Mason shrugged with his good shoulder. "Is that it?"

Frustrated at his apparent lack of concern, she clenched her fists. "Yes! That's basically it! But come on, Mason, there's got to be more. Bethany wouldn't just disappear like this. I'm really afraid she's in trouble, hurt…or worse." Just saying the words nearly brought her to her knees. "And then, there was the thing taped to my door last night," she whispered.

His eyes sharpened. "What thing?"

Rummaging in her purse, she pulled out the yearbook page. "This."

He took it from her and his brows shot up as he studied it. "And it was taped to your door?"

She nodded. "I was up pacing and praying and just… I couldn't sleep. Mom and Dad were upstairs sleeping and I didn't want to disturb them so I went downstairs. I heard something at the door and thought it was Bethany. When I opened it, that was there."

"This is a picture of us."

"Along with twenty other students who were involved in building the homecoming float."

"Still, you're right. It's kind of weird that someone would tape this to your door. I wish you hadn't touched it. I doubt we'd be able to get any prints off of it now. We'll take it in and see what the lab can find—after we convince someone to do some serious investigating." He left for a minute and came back with the page in a brown paper bag. "Might as well protect it as much as possible from here on out. They'll need to take your prints to rule them out."

"Fine. Whatever it takes. I just want to *do* something, have *somebody* doing something. Now."

Mason studied her and sighed. "All right. I can see why you're concerned, but I still want to know why you've come to me. Why ask me for help now after all these years with no contact?" He held up his hands, and for the first time since entering his house she thought she saw pain in his light blue eyes.

She had to tell him.

"Because, not only are you in that picture that was left on my door, Mason, you're the man I promised Bethany she could meet. You're her father."

TWO

Mason's knees nearly gave out. He fumbled for the chair behind him and sank onto it. Staring, he searched his mind for a response and came up blank.

A daughter? Him?

When she'd said she had a fifteen-year-old daughter, he'd immediately assumed his best friend from high school, Daniel Ackerman, was the father. But to hear her say that he was the father was almost more than he could process. In fact, the ringing in his ears made him wonder if he'd heard her right.

The expression on her face said he had.

"She's my…" He couldn't say the word.

Lacey blinked against the tears, but he noticed they just kept coming. He couldn't even think to offer her another tissue. "Yeah, Mason. She's your daughter."

"And you're just telling me this now?" he whispered. Did he even believe her? Searching her face, he could find no hint of deception or guile. Just desperation. And shame.

Then those emotions disappeared and anger made her voice hard as she ground out, "I tried to tell you sixteen years ago, but you wouldn't listen to a word I had to say, remember?"

Mason clenched his fists as he remembered their final confrontation. Her tears, Daniel's guilty flush. Mason's unwillingness to look at her, much less listen to anything she had to say. Because she'd done what he'd expected all along. Betrayed him. Just like his mother had betrayed his father and her entire family.

"All right, look." His brain struggled to adjust to all the information it had just been bombarded with. Life-changing information. "You said Bethany is missing. Let's put the past aside and focus on her."

A daughter, his mind echoed. He had a daughter.

Maybe.

If she was really his.

But what if she was?

He couldn't help wondering what she looked like. What did she think about him? Why would Lacey tell him he was the father, if he wasn't? Then again, this was the girl he'd caught in his best friend's arms and she'd denied what was before his very eyes. He didn't know what to believe, but if the possibility that their one-time intimate prom night encounter resulted in a child…

He had to know.

"I agree," she said, interrupting the endless questions he suddenly had. Relief written clearly on her strained features, she also looked grateful. "Please."

"But this issue is far from resolved."

"I know," she whispered and looked away.

Mason stood, rotated his healing shoulder, wincing at the pinch and slight stiffness, then realized his resolve to do whatever it took to get it back into tip-top shape before he returned to work just fell to second place on his priority list.

Finding his daughter had just careened its way to the top spot.

Running a hand through the hair he'd just washed before finding Lacey on his doorstep, he said, "All right, first things first. We need find out who saw her last. And if you think her disappearance has something to do with the car accident, then we need to revisit that, too."

Lacey rubbed her nose. "I'm sure Georgia knows something. I've called her several times and she swears she doesn't know where Bethany is, but I think she's hiding something." She clenched a fist and smacked her thigh. "I just can't get her to tell me anything. And the police refuse—" She broke off again and Mason could tell she was having a hard time keeping it together. She was obviously exhausted.

He had a feeling a few sleepless nights were in his immediate future, too. "Grab your stuff. Let's go talk to Georgia."

Gathering her bag and the picture, she stood. "She's probably in school."

"Then let's get her out of class."

"What do we do after that?"

"Visit the police station and see what we can find out about the wreck."

Stepping outside his home, headed for the car, Lacey did her best to shove the hurt down. Old memories threatened to overwhelm her. The fear of finding out she was pregnant. Mason's rejection...

As Mason circled the car to open the passenger door, he paused.

The sudden tense set of his shoulders set off her internal alarms. "What is it?"

His arm reached across the windshield to pull something out from under the wiper blade. "This." He held it by the very edge of one corner.

Stepping around him to look at the object in his hand, she gasped. "Another picture? Of us? That's from the yearbook, too! What's going on? How did someone know I'd be coming here?"

"Get in the car."

Eyes peeled behind him for any movement or suspicious person, he opened the door and practically shoved her in. Then he bolted around to the driver's side. He set the picture on the dash and got on the phone as he pulled out of the driveway.

Lacey listened to him bark orders and ask questions of an unidentified person as she watched the familiar scenery whiz by, but her brain didn't process it. She was too busy begging God for her daughter's life. And thanking Him that Mason had agreed to help her.

And he'd agreed before he'd found the picture on his car. Who was doing this? Was the person following them even now?

She looked in the side mirror, but saw no cars behind them. The fact didn't comfort her. She had a feeling things had just gotten started with Bethany's disappearance and whoever had left the pictures. The thought made her stomach roll.

He hung up and looked at her. "I've called Detective Catelyn Santino. She's a homicide detective…" At her gasp, he broke off then rushed to reassure her. "No, it's okay. She also investigates other stuff, too, depending on her caseload. She said she could help out with this one."

He made another phone call and Lacey heard him trying to arrange with his boss to be officially on the case. Finding fugitives was only one part of a marshal's duties. Would the powers that be let him search for a missing teen who hadn't done anything wrong and had possibly been kidnapped? Would they let him search for the person who'd left the pictures?

He hung up.

"Well?" The word popped from her mouth. She noticed he didn't tell his boss it was his own child he wanted to look for. Interesting. He was probably still in shock.

Frustration chiseled his features into a block of stone. "My boss won't officially assign me the case, although he can't dictate what I do with my time off the clock. Technically, I'm not cleared to go back to work for another couple of weeks, but that doesn't matter. Bethany will have my full attention until we get her home. And in spite of the fact that you didn't think the cops took you seriously, they did their job and filed her as a missing person."

"They did?" Tears clogged her throat and she cleared it. "I really didn't think they'd do anything. I thought they probably just stuck her information on a desk somewhere and figured she was a runaway who'd come home later."

A grim smile crossed his lips. "They may have thought about it, but they're taking it a little more seriously now. Especially when I explained about the two pictures. We'll turn them over to the investigating detectives as soon as we get there."

"How did you get them to do that? To listen to you?"

He slanted her a glance. "I'm a marshal, Lacey, I do have some pull in law enforcement, you know." He sighed. "Catelyn's going to ask to be assigned to Bethany's disappearance and doesn't think it'll be a problem. Her husband, Joseph, is FBI and an expert in finding missing people. She's contacting him, too. Before we go to the high school, she wants to talk to you."

He paused and Lacey looked at him suspiciously. "That's great. Finally, we're getting some attention. So, what's wrong?"

His fingers tightened around the steering wheel. "Catelyn has a new partner."

At the brooding look on his face, she knew. Swallowing the sudden surge of nausea, she asked, "Daniel Ackerman?"

"Yes," he clipped out, then blurted, "Is Bethany why you left town?"

She froze. Did she want to get into this now? "Lacey?"

His tight tone warned her this wasn't going to be easy. She sighed and looked at him. At his strong hands curled around the steering wheel. What was easy was remembering how much she'd loved him.

How it felt to have those fingers curled around hers, pulling her along behind him down by the lake where they used to sneak off to trade sweet kisses.

How cherished she felt when he cupped her chin to bring her lips to his….

She blinked against the rush of tears. "Yes. Mostly." But also because she'd been forced into it by parents who were ashamed their only child had gotten pregnant, that she had become a statistic her father preached against with alarming regularity.

So, yes, she'd left because of Bethany and Daniel and what Mason had believed her capable of. She'd also been devastated, crushed.

And so lonely, she'd wanted to die. She'd missed him so much, especially in the first few years of Bethany's life. But the fact that he'd dismissed her love so easily, had believed lies about her so readily, had nearly destroyed her.

She clamped her lips together and looked out the window. Since being back in town, she'd managed to avoid running into Daniel. She'd had a couple of close calls, but each time had spotted him before he'd spotted her and she'd escaped undetected.

Now, none of that mattered. None of it. Bethany was all that mattered and finding her was where she'd keep her focus.

He simply grunted and much to her relief said nothing more.

The drive to the station ended a tense silence. Lacey looked up at the building and prayed the people inside had the ability to find Bethany… alive.

As she walked into the building, Lacey felt hope tremble inside her. *Please, God,* she silently prayed. *Please use these people to lead us to Bethany.*

The air-conditioning was a blessed relief from the June heat, and she relished the coolness blowing across her skin.

Then she felt guilty. Was Bethany hot? Sweating and dreaming of a glass of water? Was she in pain? Did she need a doctor?

Was she even alive?

Once again tears sprang to the surface and she quickly shoved those thoughts aside.

"Come in here. It's an interrogation room, but we can use it," Mason said as he motioned her in. "Catelyn said she and Joseph would meet us here."

"So they're officially investigating everything, right?"

"Yes. And so is Daniel, of course."

"Of course," she murmured. She prayed she could keep her cool when Daniel appeared in front of her. Prayed she wouldn't say anything she shouldn't.

Mason pulled out the chair for her and she slid

into it. The spicy scent of his aftershave tugged at her. Just breathing it in brought back memories that caused both joy and pain.

A light tingling at the nape of her neck caused her to turn and look up at him. The flush on his cheeks gave him away. He'd reverted to an old gesture he'd had when they were dating. Pulling her hair up from her collar, brushing his fingers against her neck.

Her breathing hitched and she almost couldn't look away from him. Then he broke eye contact as the door opened and Catelyn stepped into the room.

She smiled at Mason. "Glad to see you've recovered."

"For all intents and purposes." He gestured to Lacey. "This is Lacey Gibson."

Catelyn smiled a sympathetic welcome and shook Lacey's hand. "Joseph and Daniel will be here soon." She sat opposite Mason and Lacey.

No sooner had she taken a seat when the door opened again and the man she assumed to be Joseph entered. Dark hair and dark eyes set off his Italian features. Lacey thought she could understand why Catelyn had fallen for the good-looking FBI agent and married him.

Then they were asking her for her story once again. She repeated exactly what she'd told Mason, leaving nothing out and then added the information about the note that had appeared on his car.

Mason took over from there. "I want to be in on this."

Joseph studied him then nodded. "Sure. How much time do you have before you have to be back at work?"

"Long enough to help y'all find Bethany."

Lacey wondered why he hadn't told them Bethany was his daughter. Should she mention it?

Immediately, she decided not to say anything. That would be Mason's call.

Catelyn leaned forward. "Daniel Ackerman is my partner now and he'll be helping, too. He got called away right before you arrived so I'll fill him in later. Do you have a recent picture?"

Lacey nodded and reached into her purse. She'd hoped she wouldn't need the five-by-seven print. The one she'd chosen just in case she needed to have flyers printed up. Chilled, she shivered. Never in a million years would she have imagined she'd be in this situation.

Just looking at the photo choked her throat and brought an overwhelming longing to wrap her arms around her girl.

Catelyn took the picture out and she felt Mason shift so he could see it. His gasp sent her heart thudding.

THREE

Mason felt the breath leave him.

He no longer wondered if Bethany was his. A feminine version of himself smiled back at him. A full-body shot, the picture showed a girl who was tall and lanky, with reddish-blond hair and vivid blue eyes. She was beautiful. He could see some of her mother in her, too, like the light dusting of freckles across her nose and the shape of her face, but there was no doubt she was his.

Somehow having that confirmed made it all the more real.

He had a daughter. He wondered if she liked the same things as he did. What kind of talents did she have? What were her hobbies? What…

"Do I need to get flyers printed?" Lacey's shaky voice dropped him into the present with a thud.

Joseph nodded. "It would probably be best. You're new in town—or at least Bethany is—so it would help to have her face plastered on as many surfaces as possible."

Mason saw Lacey swallow hard. Her hand trembled as she took the picture back. Her eyes lingered on the photo before returning it to her purse.

"All right," Catelyn said. "Here's the game plan. Lacey, you said the last person to see Bethany was probably Georgia Boyles. She's who we need to start with."

Mason glanced at the wall clock. "Summer school's almost over. If we get over there within the next thirty minutes, we can catch her." He looked at Lacey. "Does she walk, drive or ride the bus?"

"She drives. A blue Mustang, I think."

Joseph blew out a breath. "All right. I'll work on things from this end." He looked at Mason. "You and Catelyn can work the field if you're willing."

"Oh, I'm willing." He was more than willing. In fact, no one had better try to stop him.

And if the look on Lacey's face was any indication, she wasn't going to be left behind, either. Her arguments with Catelyn proved him right. "I'm going." Her jaw jutted and she narrowed her eyes. "I'll just follow you, if you won't let me go."

Catelyn sighed. "I could have you arrested for obstruction."

At this, Lacey's throat bobbed. "Then I'll post

bail and keep going." She sighed. "Look, I promise I won't be in the way. I just have to do this."

"Don't you have a job?"

"Yes, but I've already called and requested some time off. Finding Bethany is all that matters. I have my cell phone. If she calls, she'll call that."

Catelyn finally gave in, albeit grudgingly, and the three of them headed for their cars. Mason didn't want to leave his vehicle behind so Catelyn drove separately. Lacey rode with him. Interesting—he'd have thought she'd have taken the opportunity to put some space between them and climbed in with Catelyn.

Then again, she had come to him for help. To find her daughter. His daughter. He was having a hard time wrapping his mind around the fact, but the picture cinched it for him. Bethany was his.

Mason followed Catelyn to the high school. As it came into view, memories he thought he'd buried hit him. Hard.

He pulled into the office parking lot and turned off the engine. Lacey bolted from the vehicle as though she couldn't get out fast enough. She must have been flooded with the same memories.

Then she paused, her eyes locked on something in the distance.

"What is it?" he asked.

"Across the street, there's a photo shop. If I

hurry, I could get some flyers printed and get back to hang them around the high school before the bell rings."

"That might be a good idea."

She fixed him with a determined stare. "But you'll tell me everything Georgia tells you?"

"Everything. I promise."

She nodded. "All right. I'll try to be back within thirty minutes."

"I've got my cell phone. Just call and I'll tell you where we are. You want a ride?"

"No, it's not that far."

He shrugged. "All right. If we get done before you're ready, I'll pick you up at the shop."

She nodded and her gaze softened as she opened her mouth to say something else. She must have thought twice about it because she snapped her lips together, turned on her heel and headed across the street for the photo shop.

Lacey wanted to hurry. She wanted to get back and find out what Georgia had to say about Bethany. But she knew the faster she got these flyers printed, the faster she'd have Bethany's face plastered around the city. And beyond if necessary.

She pushed open the glass door that had enough flyers taped on it to wallpaper her bathroom and entered the store. She jumped when the bell rang to announce her presence. A clerk who looked to be in his mid-fifties and needing a shave came to the counter. "Can I help you?"

"I need to print some flyers. My daughter is missing and I need to get the flyers put up as soon as possible." She pulled the picture out and handed it to him.

He frowned down at Bethany's picture. "I'm sure sorry to hear that. I'll be glad to get these printed. You want to add her name and a contact phone number on here?"

Of course, why hadn't she thought of that? She was so frazzled! "Um, yes. That would be great."

Get it together, Lacey, Bethany's counting on you.

"Won't take me a minute to scan it into the computer, add the information and then get everything printed up. I'll do it as a rush job for you."

Lacey felt tears mist her eyes. "Thanks, I appreciate that."

She gave him the information to add to the flyers and while the clerk went to work in the back room, she paced back and forth in front of the counter, thinking of the different locations she could put the flyers. Locations that offered the best traffic where the most people would see it.

A shadow passed by the door and she turned, expecting to see someone enter.

No one did.

She went back to her pacing.

Again, movement by the glass door caught her attention. Strange movement, like someone bobbing up and down.

Thinking someone needed help opening the heavy door, she walked over to it, and pulled it open. No one was there.

Huh, that's odd.

Just to make sure, she stepped outside to look to the right.

Nothing.

As she looked to the left, something slammed into her lower back propelling her against the wall. The breath left her so fast, she couldn't even scream. In shock, she felt her face scrape the side of the building.

Before she could gather her stunned wits, a voice whispered in her ear, "She's mine now and you'll never find her."

Fear careened through her and she struggled to turn around on legs that felt like jelly. Her face burned and her back felt bruised.

The blue sky turned dark and for a moment she was afraid she would pass out.

Running footsteps echoed back to her, mocking her, letting her know she was helpless. With a frustrated and angry cry, she slid down the wall to sit on the ground and weep for her lost child.

* * *

Mason ground his teeth in frustration at Georgia's refusal to cooperate. The fact that she even had to attend the summer session due to a flunking grade in English had already spiked her attitude. Being questioned about a wreck she claimed to have nothing to do with sent it skyrocketing.

Her wide gray eyes flicked back and forth between the three adults staring at her. Her lips clamped together in a tight snarl. Mason thought they might need a blowtorch to pry them apart.

The principal had asked to stay in the room. Since Georgia was over fourteen, they didn't need parental permission to question the girl although they had given her mother a courtesy call.

She was on the way.

He briefly wondered how Lacey was doing, then focused his attention back to Bethany's stubborn friend. Her body language and uncomfortable shifting when questioned about the wreck all suggested she was lying about not being there.

He leaned forward. "Look, Bethany's missing. From all appearances, she wouldn't run away. In fact, from what her mother says, she was scared of something, nervous all the time. She felt like her life might be in danger. That, coupled with her disappearance, sends up a big red flag. She might be counting on you to help find her."

Georgia licked her lips. Some of the attitude

faded as she finally looked him straight in the eye. "I don't know where she is, I promise!"

Deflated, he realized he believed her. She didn't know where Bethany was. But she sure knew something. "What are you afraid to tell me? To tell us?"

Georgia jumped to her feet. "Nothing! There's nothing to tell!" Tears leaked down her cheeks and she palmed them away leaving black streaks of mascara behind. "If I could help you find Bethany, I would. But you're right about one thing. She was scared of someone."

"Who?"

The girl slumped back into the chair and slapped a hand on the table. "I don't know! I wish I did, but I just don't. But she can take care of herself. She's got a first-degree black belt in karate, you know?"

Mason started. Lacey hadn't mentioned that. "What?"

"Yeah, she's like addicted. Does all kinds of competitions—and wins. So she can handle whatever comes along." Frustration slid over her face. "But I don't know where she's hiding out. I promise."

"Hiding out?" Mason jumped on those two words. "So she left on her own?"

Georgia groaned. "No! I don't know! I don't know what she's doing or where she is. She didn't say anything about leaving before she disappeared. That much I do know."

Catelyn blew out a sigh and looked over at Mason. He shook his head. They weren't going to get anything from Georgia. However, he had to ask, "Were you with Kayla the night of the accident?"

"No! Why do people keep asking me that? No! I wasn't there, all right?" Her breath came in pants and sweat broke across her upper lip.

She was lying. But he wasn't going to get her to admit it. Yet. "All right, thanks for meeting with us." He slipped her his card. "But if you think of anything at all, will you please call me?"

"Sure." She slipped the card into her back pocket.

Mason stopped her. "Do you feel like you're in any danger, Georgia? Because I can help, if you do."

"No," she mumbled. "I'm not in any danger. Now I gotta go." She escaped the room as fast as she could. Her mother hadn't even arrived yet.

Mason looked at Catelyn. "She's definitely scared."

"But of what? Of who?"

"I don't know, but I think Lacey may have been on to something when she said that Bethany's disappearance had something to do with the car accident. Georgia was involved in it—no matter how adamantly she denies it—and she's scared to death about something. Bethany was probably with the two girls, too, and now she's missing."

"Kayla is dead, Bethany's missing and Georgia's scared. I think I'm going to have an officer keep an eye on her for her own safety."

Mason tapped his chin and watched Georgia disappear into the throng of students ready to get out of the building and go do something fun. "I think that's a good idea. I also think we need to revisit that accident. Who was the lead investigator in it?"

"My partner. Daniel Ackerman."

Mason felt his gut clench. He hadn't spoken more than three sentences to Daniel since the day he'd caught Lacey kissing his friend. Even though it wasn't Daniel's fault that Lacey had come on to him, the man was a reminder of one of the most painful times of his life.

And even though Daniel had married and moved on, Mason couldn't get the betrayal out of his mind.

"Fine," he muttered. "Then let's find Daniel and get all of the evidence about the accident back out. I want everything sent back to the lab. Since it was ruled an accident, the forensics people probably didn't go over everything quite as thoroughly as they would a murder."

"If that car wreck wasn't an accident, then it was murder."

"Yeah." His phone rang and he saw Lacey's number pop up. His heart squeezed. "Hello?"

"Mason?" Her shaky voice put him on instant alert.

"What is it, Lacey?"

"I was attacked." She sobbed. He heard her trying to catch her breath. "But I think I have something to add to the investigation. Can you come?"

Heart in his throat, he promised to be there in less than a minute. He looked at Catelyn. "Come on, this is a police matter."

He raced from the room, Catelyn following along behind him, his mind looping with Lacey's first three words, *I was attacked*...and realized with some surprise that he wanted to hurt the person who'd hurt her.

Forty-five seconds later, when he saw her sitting against the side of the building with an ice pack on her cheek, the rage inside him tripled and he knew without a doubt that past or no past, betrayal or no betrayal, he was going to fall for Lacey Gibson once again.

And wondered how he was going to keep his heart from being ripped in two when it happened.

FOUR

Lacey pressed the ice pack to her head and stood. The feel of Mason's solid grip on her upper arm scrambled her brain more than the knock against the side of the building.

He and Catelyn had arrived almost immediately, the poor store owner having time only to offer his help and fix the ice pack, which she insisted she didn't need.

He insisted she did.

The print shop owner stood with the pictures of Bethany clutched in his left hand as he attempted to answer Catelyn's questions. "I'm sorry, I didn't see anything. I don't usually have any problems around here."

Lacey shook her head and winced. "It wasn't your fault. Whoever it was knew exactly who they were attacking."

"Why do you say that?" Mason frowned.

"Because he specifically said, 'She's mine

now.' Who else would he be referring to except Bethany?"

His frown deepened. "Did you see him? What was the voice like?"

Squinting against the throbbing in her head, she replayed the scene in her mind. With a shudder, she swallowed. "No, I didn't see him. Just a glimpse. And his voice was low, raspy, like someone with a bad cold…." She shrugged. "I don't know. I'm sure the person disguised his voice."

Mason sighed and guided her over to the car. "We need to get your head checked out."

She waved him away. "It's fine. Just a bump and a scrape." It hurt, but she didn't have time to deal with it now. She scrambled back out of the car. "I forgot the flyers."

Before he could stop her, Lacey made her way back up the store owner. He handed the package to her. "Take them."

Lacey reached for her wallet—another indication the attack had had a specific purpose. He'd left her purse when he could have easily snatched it.

A hand on her arm brought her gaze up and she looked into the man's kind eyes. "No, ma'am. This is my gift, my part to help you find your daughter."

Tears choked her once again and she stared at him through the blur. "Thank you."

Mason placed an arm around her shoulders and steered her back toward the car. "Now, let's get you checked out."

Weariness tugged at her now that the adrenaline had faded. However, Bethany came first. "I'm not going to a doctor." She shivered. "Somehow, deep down in my bones, I feel like time is running out for Bethany. We need to find her now."

A frown creased his brows. "All right, but if you start feeling sick, I want you to tell me. Promise?"

His concern set off all kinds of warm sensations in the depths of her being. She swallowed hard and steeled herself against the longing just being around him stirred up. "Promise."

Catelyn joined them at the car. "All right. I think we've done all we can do here. I'm going to see if any of the security cameras around here picked up anything."

Mason nodded. "I want to look at the investigation file from the wreck."

"You'll have to talk to Daniel. He was the lead investigator on that one and will be able to help you out there."

Lacey bit her lip and shot Mason a look even as she thought that Daniel might be *able* to help them, but would he?

Mason cleared his throat. "I'll talk to him."

A ringing phone made her jump. Then she

realized it was hers. Bethany? Yanking it from her pocket, she glanced at the caller ID and bit her lip as a wave of grief nearly knocked her over. Not Bethany. "Hi, Mom."

"Have you heard anything?"

Her parents had accepted both of them back into their lives with open arms. As always, guilt pierced her. She'd been so wrong to keep Bethany from people who would have loved her. And yet, they'd been the ones to send her off in the beginning and it had taken her a long time to get past that.

When they'd started begging for reconciliation by Bethany's sixth birthday, Lacey had enough bitterness and resentment flowing that she'd repeatedly refused.

Until God got ahold of her three years ago, after her landlady led her to know Christ.

Clearing her throat, she turned from Mason and Catelyn and faced the car. "Not yet, Mom, but Mason agreed to help me."

A pause. "Did you tell him?"

"Yes."

"How did he take it?"

"Um…better than I expected, I think. Actually, I'm not really sure yet. Can I get back to you on that one?"

A sigh filtered through the line. "Of course." Lacey thought she heard her mother stifle a sob, then she cleared her throat and reported, "Your boss called. He wants to know exactly how long you plan to be gone."

Anger at the man rose up inside her and she turned to see Mason and Catelyn deep in discussion. Louder than she wanted, she blurted, "I'm not sure, Mom. As long as it takes, all right?" Mason's head lifted at her tone and he lifted a brow at her.

She closed her eyes and dropped her head. She'd just started a new job as a graphic artist. A big project sat on her desk and she knew her boss was concerned about getting it done by the deadline.

In a quieter voice, she said, "If he calls back, tell him I'll try to get to it as soon as I know I can't do anything else for Bethany here—or we have her back. I need to go. I'll call you if I find anything out."

"Will you be here for supper?"

Lacey met Mason's gaze and her heart thudded. "I don't know. I'll let you know a little later this afternoon, all right?"

"Fine. Keep me posted, darling."

"I will."

Lacey hung up and leaned against the open door of the vehicle. Mason and Catelyn walked over. Catelyn held out a hand. "If you'll give me the flyers, I'll ask some of Bethany's classmates if they'll hang them up around the school and town."

"Sure." Bethany peeled off half the papers and gave them to Catelyn. "Thank you so much."

The detective smiled. "No problem." Then she looked at Mason. "I'll be in touch."

Mason nodded then leaned over and placed a hand on the roof next to Lacey's head. "Who was on the phone?"

"My mother. She's worried, but I can tell she's not quite sure Bethany didn't just take off. I know she didn't but Mom's not convinced."

"Why's that?"

Lacey blew out a sigh and shook her head, wincing at the sting incited by her hair moving across the scraped area on her cheek. Gentle fingers reached out and removed the strands. The breath left her lungs and she just stared at the man before her.

He blinked and curled his fingers into a fist at his side. Sorrow for what might have been pained her. "Bethany's threatened it more than once. Said she was tired of waiting around on me to—" she sucked in a deep breath and let it out slow "—to get up the guts to tell you about her and she wasn't sticking around if I wasn't going to come through."

Mason turned his back on her and placed his hands on his hips. She'd seen the flash of fury before he'd hidden his eyes. The fact that she probably deserved it didn't lessen the hurt. "I'm sorry," she whispered. "I know now I was wrong."

"Why were you so hesitant to tell her about me? What did you think I would do?"

"I didn't know what you would or wouldn't do! When you believed the lies Daniel told you, all of a sudden you weren't who I thought you were. How did I know you wouldn't accuse Bethany of lying to you? How did I know you wouldn't break her heart and send her home permanently damaged because of your rejection?"

He whirled back to her, the agonizing hurt in his eyes nearly undoing her. But she held her ground. He'd wanted the truth. Now he had it.

His lips moved but nothing came out. The tense set of his jaw said he was biting his tongue. Then he simply whispered, "How could you think that of me?"

She sighed. "After what you put me through, how could I think anything else?" When he closed his eyes, she decided to change the subject. "All that aside, Mason, she wouldn't willingly leave home. Bethany would never do that."

"How do you know, Lacey?" He opened his eyes, but narrowed them at her. His soft tone couldn't hide the steel undercurrent in his words.

"Because I know Bethany. She was full of empty threats, but she would never go off on her own." Biting her lower lip, she wondered if she should tell him exactly why. Bethany would be mortified if she ever found out Lacey shared one of her deepest, darkest secrets with him.

But she would if it meant convincing him. Even her parents didn't know Bethany's secret.

Without another word, he simply motioned for her to get in the car.

Once they were buckled and heading away from the school, she asked, "Where are we going?"

"To the station. I want to talk to Daniel."

She gulped and looked out the window.

"Tell me something about her," he said suddenly.

She knew what he meant. He wanted her to tell him something that would help him get to know his daughter a little better.

"She's always comparing herself to a missing puzzle piece." Lacey wasn't sure why she picked that particular fact to share, but it seemed right.

"What?"

Lacey breathed a little laugh, wishing she could inject some humor in it. "She says that sometimes her life feels like a puzzle, but there's a piece missing."

"Me?"

"I asked her that, and she said that was part of it, but she said she just never seems to be able to find her niche. Where she fits."

"She found friends here." He looked confused.

"She did. From the time Bethany turned seven, we had to move around a lot in North Carolina." She shrugged. "I didn't like it, but I had to go where I could find a job. Several times my job only lasted a year or two and we'd move again. Then finally we moved here." She shrugged. "I guess she's just missing some roots maybe."

"Maybe."

"The one good thing that came from moving here is she finally found friends in Kayla and Georgia. And while she and Georgia are great buddies, she just really seemed to connect with Kayla from the moment they met." Lacey gave a sad smile. "She said they got along so well because they were like two pieces missing from their completed puzzle and until they found where they fit or where they belonged, they would love and support each other. BFFs."

"They sound like a couple of great kids."

"They are. I mean, Bethany is and Kayla was." She bit her lip. "I still can't believe she's dead some days. And poor Bethany. She was just devastated. She started spending all of her free time at the karate school."

"Georgia mentioned something about that. How long has she been studying martial arts?"

"From the time she was three. We were at a spring festival one afternoon and a karate school had a demonstration. She was riveted and begged to take lessons. Finally, I gave in and signed her up. That was one thing I made sure of before we moved. That wherever we wound up had to have a dojo, or marital arts school. Fortunately, I never had to move too far from where we started out and she was able to go to the same karate school for a long time. It was worth the drive to keep some consistency in her life." Lacey rubbed her eyes. "I think her being able to focus on the martial arts helped her get through a lot of emotional stuff. When Kayla died, Bethany spent even more time at the dojo."

Mason raised a brow and said, "Then we need to talk to all of the kids at the school. The ones she had class with or hung out with."

Lacey flushed. "I don't know if it would do any good. She wasn't close to any of them. She said most of the students there weren't serious about the sport and played too much."

Lifting his phone to his ear, he spoke into it. "Catelyn, we need to question Bethany's instructor and classmates at the karate school on Brownstock Road. Lacey said Bethany spent a lot of time there."

He must have gotten an affirmative response because he hung up. When he spoke again, he changed the subject. "Sounds like she's been through a lot lately. Honestly, if it wasn't for those weird pictures showing up at each of our respective houses and the fact that you were just attacked, I might be inclined to agree with your mother."

"But you don't."

A tense hand curled around the steering wheel. She watched the color fade from his knuckles. A muscle jumped in his cheek. "No, I don't. It all seems too weird to be coincidental. And the attacker basically confirmed that Bethany met with foul play by what he said to you."

"Yeah." She swallowed hard and felt the tears gather. Foul play. She sure didn't like the sound of that. Especially not when it was used in conjunction with her missing daughter.

Mason pulled into the police station parking lot. Lacey climbed out and felt dread cramp her stomach. Daniel Ackerman was inside. He was the last man on the planet she wanted to face.

But for Bethany, she'd do it.

FIVE

Mason kept the smile in place as Daniel walked toward them. With one hand on Lacey's upper arm, he could feel her muscles tense.

A fine tremor shook her, but she held her head high and met Daniel's gaze with a classiness Mason grudgingly admired.

He wished the memories of the last time the three of them had been in the same area would quit bombarding him. Renewed anger flooded him as old feelings of betrayal and soul-searing hurt came back with a vengeance.

With superhuman effort, he pushed aside his emotions and watched the approaching man.

When Daniel caught sight of Lacey and recognized her, shock flashed and he gave a slight stumble.

Interesting.

"Lacey Gibson?"

"Hello, Daniel." Her voice was low. If he hadn't

been listening for it, Mason would have missed the slight wobble.

Daniel paused to offer a hand to Mason. Mason shook it then felt like excusing himself to find some soap and water. Instead, he got right to the point. "Lacey's daughter is missing."

"Bethany Gibson is *your* daughter?" Daniel had gathered his usual cool demeanor back and his face now showed no expression other than professional concern. He looked at Lacey. "You've heard nothing from her?"

"Nothing." The clipped, one-word answer told Mason Lacey was on shaky ground. However it didn't stop her from pulling a folded piece of paper from her purse and handing it over to the man.

Daniel took it and Mason nodded toward Daniel's office. "Can we talk?"

Daniel hesitated, looked Lacey up and down as though trying to convince himself she was really standing there, then said, "Sure, come on back."

Once in the office, Lacey seated herself on the edge of the brown couch, shoulders held stiff, fingers pinched around the strap of her small purse.

Daniel cleared his throat and looked like he might say something of a personal nature then focused on the flyer in front of him. "We have a missing persons report filed and we have officers keeping an eye out for her based on the picture you provided when you filed the report. I don't really know what else you want us to do."

Mason laid a hand on Lacey's arm before she could come out of her seat and tell the man exactly what she wanted him to do. She shifted but stayed quiet. Mason looked at his former friend. "We want you to reopen the case of the car accident that happened back at the beginning of April."

"The one where Kayla Mahoney was killed," Lacey blurted.

Daniel sat back and raised his brows. They'd managed to surprise him. "Why?"

Mason took over. "Because she was friends with Bethany. We talked to Georgia, the girl who Lacey thinks was in the car that night with Kayla, but she denies it vehemently."

"And she says they weren't with Kayla that night," Lacey offered.

Mason glanced at Lacey. "But Lacey thinks they were, even though Bethany denied it when confronted a few weeks ago."

The detective shrugged. "Then what makes you think Bethany and Georgia are lying?"

"Because they're scared."

"Of what?"

This time Lacey did jump up. "If we knew that, my daughter might not be missing!"

Daniel didn't react, simply leaned forward, keeping his eyes on Mason. "That wreck was ruled an accident. Catelyn and I both investigated it. A simple one-car accident caused by a reckless teen."

"And you proved that without a doubt? You had the crime-scene guys go over the car with a fine-tooth comb?"

A flush climbed up the man's neck to settle on his cheeks. "Look, that wreck was two months ago. Yes, we checked everything. Kayla lost control of the car and what happened, happened. Unfortunately, even our city isn't immune from teen-driver deaths."

"I'm not saying that, Daniel, I'm saying something's going on and Bethany's involved somehow." He repeated what Lacey had told him earlier at his house. "She was scared. Someone seemed to be after her."

Daniel stood. "That's all hearsay. I need proof."

Forcing himself to unclench his teeth, Mason held his temper. "And I'm telling you that the proof might have been in that car." A thought occurred to him. "Do you mind if we look at the report?"

"And *I'm* telling you there's no need. It was an accident."

Frustration lanced him. Why was the man fighting him so hard on this? Mason narrowed his eyes.

"Let him see the file, Daniel."

Mason and Lacey turned as one to see Catelyn standing in the door of the office.

Daniel let out a low sound of disgust and stomped to the file cabinet in the corner of the room. Tugging open a drawer, he searched until he found what he was looking for.

Turning, he slapped the file in front of Mason. "There." Fury glittered in his gaze. "I don't appreciate the insinuation that I missed something."

Ah, so that was the issue. "I'm not saying you missed something because you didn't do your job, I'm just saying a fresh set of eyes might not be a bad thing."

"Whatever. I'm going to get some coffee."

Catelyn stepped into the room as Daniel brushed past her. She said, "I worked the wreck with him. I don't know what you think you'll find, but have at it."

With Daniel's departure, Lacey felt as if she could breathe again. At least until Mason leaned in close to look at the file with her. His unique scent filled her senses, and she pulled it in as though clinging to that, she could have a piece of him to call her own once again.

She appreciated his support even though she knew he still wanted to discuss the past— and Bethany. However, his priority—finding

Bethany—matched hers at the moment and she was grateful.

Mason pulled pictures of the wreck from the file and spread them on Daniel's desk. Lacey stood to get a better view.

When he unveiled pictures of the dead teen still seated behind the wheel, Lacey gasped and turned away from the photo, nausea swirling in her gut.

"Sorry," Mason offered. "Let me sort through them. Don't look until I tell you to."

Gathering her emotions and clamping them under control, she turned back. "No, I need to see them all."

"Lacey..."

"Just show me."

With a heavy sigh, Mason did as she asked and placed them in the order they'd been shot. Gulping a fortifying breath, Lacey studied each photo, throwing up mental blocks that this was a girl she'd had in her home, taken to eat pizza and was Bethany's best friend. She forced herself to go over every detail even as her heart broke for the precious life cut short.

Oh, Bethany, where are you? *Please, God, don't let Bethany be dead. Keep her in Your care wherever she is.*

She studied the interior of the car, the exterior, the shadows behind the vehicle.

And then she saw it.

Another gasp slipped from her as she grabbed Mason's arm without thinking. "There. Isn't that a gold necklace on the ground beside the back door?"

Mason moved in for a closer look. The warmth of his bare forearm burned her hand and she snatched it back, curling her fingers into a fist. Before, she would have rubbed her hand up and down his arm in a soothing, affectionate motion, then end with entwining his fingers with hers.

Now she didn't have that right.

"It looks like it."

Catelyn and Daniel returned to the office just as Mason picked up the picture. He looked at Daniel. "Do you have a magnifying glass?"

Without comment, the man rounded his desk and pulled open his top drawer. "Here."

"Thanks." Mason held the glass over the area of the picture Lacey had pointed out to him. "Yeah, that's a gold chain all right." He looked at Daniel. "Can we get this blown up?"

"Why?"

"Because," Lacey answered, "Bethany had a gold chain she wore all the time. She never took it off. I noticed shortly after the wreck it was gone. When I asked her what happened to it, she said the clasp had broken at school and she'd lost it."

Daniel shrugged. "Sounds reasonable to me."

Frustration filled her. "Yes, I thought so too and

didn't think anything more about it, but the more I look at that chain, the more I think it might be hers."

"How would you identify it? There must be a zillion gold chains out there."

"But not with a puzzle piece attached to it. She had one half and Kayla had the other half. They each had their names engraved on it along with *BFF.*"

"Meaning Best Friends Forever," Mason murmured.

"Right." She reached for the pictures still laid out on the desk, sorted through them, then pulled one from the pile. "Look, you can see Kayla's wearing hers here."

Catelyn took the other picture containing the shot of the gold necklace from the desk. "Follow me."

Hope making her heart pound like crazy, Lacey didn't hesitate, but hurried after the woman. She felt Mason's presence right behind her. And Daniel's.

She shuddered. When she'd first caught sight of the man walking toward her, she'd wanted to demand that he tell Mason the truth about what had really happened sixteen years ago, but had nearly bitten her tongue off to keep the words from flying from her mouth.

Now wasn't the time.

This wasn't about her and Mason—or even Daniel. This was about Bethany. She knew a confrontation with Daniel was coming at some point, though.

And soon.

Catelyn led them into another room that looked like a small lab. "Normally, we use the big lab downtown or send stuff off to Columbia, but this little area was funded by an anonymous donor. One tool we have is a highly efficient microscope that will enable us to get a good look at this chain."

She maneuvered her way to the device and slid the picture under the glass. After flipping a few switches, the image appeared on the oversize computer screen in front of them.

Within seconds, Catelyn had adjusted the focus and Lacey stared at her daughter's necklace. "It's hers."

Even Mason had to admit it.

A dainty golden puzzle piece dangled from the end of a gold chain. The words *Kayla and Bethany—BFF* filled the screen.

SIX

Lacey felt the air leave her lungs. How she'd hoped she'd be wrong. But she wasn't. She felt no satisfaction in being right. "What do we do now?" She looked up at Mason. "She was there. Something happened that night other than Kayla just dying in a car accident. Something that instilled a fear in Bethany that she felt she couldn't share with me."

Mason scrubbed a hand down his cheek and sighed. He looked at Catelyn. "All right, I think this is enough evidence to prove that Lacey may be on to something, don't you?"

The detective nodded. "It's possible."

Standing, Lacey twisted her fingers together. "You have to get Georgia to tell you what they were doing that night."

"Daniel?"

They all turned at the voice in the doorway. Lacey gasped and jumped up. "Janice?"

The tall, regal-looking woman paused, her

attention swinging from Daniel to Lacey. A hand fluttered to her chest. "Lacey, darling, how are you?"

Feeling a tremulous smile hover on her lips, Lacey gave a low humorless laugh. "I've been better. My daughter is missing."

A perfectly arched brow lifted. "I'd heard you were back with a child in tow."

Unsure how to take that comment, Lacey just stared at Daniel's wife, the woman who'd once been her closest friend. Then all of the pretense seemed to slough off of Janice and her expression softened. She moved forward and clasped Lacey in a hug. "I've been terribly angry with you."

Lacey pulled back. "For what?"

"You left without a word sixteen years ago, didn't call, didn't send the first Christmas card and then came back to town without calling. What is that all about?"

How could she explain without making everyone in the room more uncomfortable? She couldn't. "I'm sorry. You're absolutely right. As soon as we get Bethany home, we'll get together, all right?" She squeezed her friend's hand. "I've missed you and thought about you often." That wasn't a lie. Upon her move back to town, she'd thought about calling Janice but when she'd found out the woman was married to Daniel Ackerman, she just couldn't bring herself to dial the number.

"Sure." Janice smoothed a nonexistent stray hair and tugged at the scarf tied in a fashionably loose knot around her neck.

Mason and Catelyn exchanged a look, and Lacey knew exactly what they were thinking. They had an investigation going on and needed to get back to it.

Daniel frowned at his wife, irritation stamped on his features. "What are you doing here? I thought you were working in the shop today? Or volunteering at the hospital or something."

"I was at the shop until the air conditioner died on me." She looked at Lacey. "I own the Christmas Every Day Shop." She grinned. "My father bought it for me."

Lacey gave a tight smile. Nothing had changed in that area. Janice was still a daddy's girl who loved to spend the man's money. And he obviously still let her.

Janice said, "I'm only open six months out of the year and I'm just three days from opening up for this year. Now this." She pursed her lips in disgust and turned back to her husband. "And you know I volunteer at the hospital on Fridays, not Tuesdays."

Daniel took a deep breath. "Right, sorry."

"Well, no matter, I'll just have to delay opening the shop a few weeks. I don't suppose it will make that much of a difference." She looked at Daniel.

"I did promise to help out at the clothes closet at the church. Martha called and said they had a new batch to sort."

Crossing his arms, Mason shifted and shot Daniel a pointed look. Daniel caught the unspoken message. To Janice, he said, "Look, hon, we're kind of in the middle of something. Call me in a couple of hours and I'll see what I can do about finding someone to fix the air conditioner. Or call Jack Durant."

Janice waved a hand in dismissal. "I'll handle it, but turn on your phone, would you? I wouldn't have to track you down if you'd answer."

With a flush, Daniel did as requested then escorted his wife from the office. When he returned, he glanced around and cleared his throat. "She could've called my office line," he muttered. "Sorry about that. The shop is sort of like her child since we can't…" He broke off and shook his head. "Never mind. Okay, so where were we?"

Lacey pulled in a deep breath. Seeing Janice and Daniel together sent pangs of unexpected— and unwanted—jealousy through her. Why did the man who'd cost her a lifetime of love and happiness get to have it? It wasn't fair.

But God never promised fair, she reminded herself, He just promised to be there with her through whatever life threw at her.

Like finding her missing daughter.

"I wish we still had that car," Mason muttered.

Catelyn lifted her head with a snap. "We do."

"What?" Mason and Lacey asked simultaneously.

"While there was only one beer bottle found at the scene, it's been ruled an alcohol-related wreck. The car's at the high school."

"Was Kayla drinking?" Mason asked, jaw tight.

Daniel shook his head. "There was no alcohol in her blood. She wasn't drinking and driving."

Lacey felt some relief flood her. But if Kayla wasn't drinking, who was? Surely not Bethany. She realized the irony of her thinking. Her own parents never would have believed she'd come home with the news she was pregnant before it had happened. So…had Bethany been drinking that night? Where did the beer bottle come from?

She may never know, she realized.

Catelyn was saying, "In spite of their grief, Kayla's parents wanted to make sure Kayla's death wasn't for nothing and donated the car for the MADD cause."

"Mothers Against Drunk Driving," Mason stated the obvious. "They do a semiannual program. One in August at the beginning of school and one in May just before school lets out."

Daniel nodded. "Right, I saw that in the paper.

They used Kayla's car this past May. They're planning on using it again this fall when school starts back."

With a forefinger, Mason tapped his lips and Lacey shivered, remembering when he used to smile at her so sweetly. On their first date, he'd kissed her knuckles, then her forehead.

He'd been such a gentleman, not like most of the guys he'd hung around with. Jerks like Daniel Ackerman.

She pushed those thoughts aside and focused on what Mason was saying. "I don't know if it would do us any good to get that car back to the lab so a forensics team could go over it."

Lacey stood and placed her hands on her hips. "It might. Surely no one's really touched the car. I mean, did they clean it up before putting it on display?"

Catelyn shook her head and grimaced. "No, the parents wanted the kids to have the full shock value if they looked at the air bag close enough. Although with the roof caved in the way it is, you can't really see much unless you're right up on it." She explained, "When the car hit the tree, the top part of the tree broke off and fell on top of the vehicle."

Lacey winced. And Bethany was possibly inside? The thought made her feel a little sick.

"And," Mason offered, "they usually display it

in front of the school with crime tape sectioning it off to keep people away from it. So, it's not unreasonable to think that the car hasn't been touched since the wreck."

"But what about the weather?" Daniel asked. "I mean it's been rained on." He shook his head. "I don't think you'd get much from forensics."

Without meaning to, Lacey let her gaze meet Daniel's. His hard brown eyes bored into hers and she shivered. What was he thinking? He'd been on edge since they'd all entered his office.

Was he afraid she'd bring up his past lies about her right there in front of everyone? She certainly wanted to. She lifted her chin and narrowed her eyes refusing to look away. He shifted first then dropped his gaze to the photos still on the table.

Mason placed a hand on her arm, and she jumped. He said to Catelyn and Daniel, "I think it's worth a try. Even being out in the elements, there still might be something on the inside. Or even in the trunk." He firmed his jaw and nodded. "Let's do it."

Catelyn shrugged. "Fine with me. I'll get the forensics people to get the car themselves and tell them what we need."

She exited the room leaving Lacey alone with the two men. Daniel notched his chin at Mason. "Why are you so interested in this case?"

Mason just looked at his friend while Lacey

held her breath. "A lot of reasons." He cut his gaze toward her. "How's your head?"

Absently, she touched her cheek then winced. "Fine. Or it will be in couple of days. So, what's the next step in finding Bethany?"

"I think we need to talk to Georgia again while we wait for the forensics team to get finished with the car."

Lacey crossed her arms and hugged herself. "Then we go back to the high school?"

Mason shook his head. "No, I think it would be best to catch her at home this time." He grabbed the pictures of Kayla's wreck and shoved them back into the folder. Placing it back on the desk, he said to Lacey, "Come on, we need to see Bethany's room. Then we can see about talking to Georgia."

When Catelyn returned, they filled her in on the plan and the foursome left the station to climb into two separate cars. Lacey and Mason into his and Catelyn and Daniel into the police vehicle.

Ten minutes later, they pulled up at the curb of Lacey's parents' house. After a brief explanation to her parents as to the reason she was home with the police in tow, Lacey led the way down the hall to Bethany's room. Her parents hovered in the background, but stayed out of the way and didn't pepper Lacey or the others with questions.

Lacey silently pushed the door open and sucked

in a deep breath. How she wanted to open the door and have Bethany fuss at her for not knocking.

Stepping inside, the detectives swept the area first with their eyes, then snapped on gloves and began going through Bethany's personal things. Mason handed her a pair of the gloves. "I guess I know better than to ask you to wait in the hall. Besides, we might have questions for you."

Lacey raised her fingers and wiggled them. "I've already been through this room a dozen times," she protested. "My fingerprints are everywhere."

Mason shrugged. "Then if we find something, we'll rule your prints out and don't have to worry about ours. And maybe we'll find something new that you haven't touched yet."

As she pulled the gloves on, her stomach clenched at the invasion of Bethany's privacy. Her daughter would have a stroke if she knew, but if it would help find her...

Mason's expression caught her attention. He looked like a kid at Christmastime who'd been told all the toys under the tree were his. She knew he was taking in every detail of Bethany's room. Only, in spite of the gloves, he was looking at it from a father's perspective instead of as a cop.

It made Lacey take another closer look at the room. After a short Goth stage, Bethany got into elegant. Gold trimmed curtains and matching bed spread, a canopy and throw rug all said *classy*. Lacey had gotten the material at a thrift store and together she and Bethany had made every piece. She sighed and stroked the comforter. She and Bethany had been so close during that time. Now...

He walked to the end table and picked up a picture. "She likes to ski?"

Lacey laughed and stood beside him, breathing in his nearness, her heart rejoicing at his presence. Then breaking at the cause of it. "Oh, Bethany..." she whispered, tracing a finger over the girl's big grin. She looked right at home on the pair of skis, the blue in the jacket making her eyes brighter than the blue of a clear summer sky. "She loves it. The lady who we rented an apartment from used to take Bethany to church where she got involved in the youth group. One year they went skiing when she was about twelve. She's been hooked ever since."

Pulling in a deep breath, he replaced the picture and moved on to the shelves over her desk. "Karate trophies."

"Yes." She grinned. "It seems like every Saturday, we were road-tripping it somewhere. She hasn't done as many competitions lately." Lacey frowned and muttered, "She hasn't wanted to."

"If you don't mind me asking, how did you

pay for it—the lessons, the competitions, everything?"

Lacey felt a flush cover her cheeks and narrowed her eyes. "I worked for it."

This time he turned red. "That's not what I meant. I just...well this is an expensive sport, I just..." He trailed off. "Sorry."

She gave him a break and decided to answer. "I worked two jobs, one from home where I could be with Bethany and then the graphics design one. With both of those, I could make ends meet and have a little left over for Bethany and I to do some fun things. Like road trips for karate competitions."

A look she thought she recognized as admiration shone briefly in his eyes. "You're an amazing mom."

Embarrassed at the unexpected praise, mostly because no one had ever told her that before, she simply gaped at him them mumbled, "Well, I don't know about that."

Mason simply smiled and moved on.

Pulling open the long thin drawer on the desk, he looked inside. Lacey looked over his shoulder. She'd already been through it and could tell him what it contained. A stack of papers, a few pens, a math book. Lacey reached around him and picked up the papers. Catelyn had finished in the closet and Daniel stood looking at the edge of the window. Absently, she wondered what he was looking at.

With a sigh, she flipped through the first few sheets. School-related announcements, one for a summer camp held in Colorado. Lacey almost chuckled. The girl had big dreams. "She wants to go to camp in Colorado," she murmured. "Why would she willingly disappear when she's dreaming about the future?"

She wouldn't.

And then the next one made her gasp.

Mason glanced at her and asked, "What is it?"

His words barely registered in the rushing roar of her fear. Hands trembling, she held out the picture.

She heard his swiftly indrawn breath as he saw it. "It's another picture from the yearbook."

A younger version of Mason and Lacey grinned back at them. A bull's-eye had been drawn over each of their faces.

At the bottom of the picture someone had taped a picture of Bethany. A full-body shot taken while Bethany lay sprawled on a bench outside the school. Her lunch tray lay on the ground beside her and it looked like she had fallen asleep. The picture itself would have been cute had it not been for the red slash someone had drawn across Bethany's throat.

SEVEN

Mason felt his skin crawl. His stomach tied itself in knots and he thought if he didn't find out who was behind all this, he might just snap.

Staring down at the picture, he felt slightly nauseous. Who would do this? What kind of enemy had Lacey made? And how? What could she have done during the short time she'd been home?

Or had someone followed her home?

He looked at Lacey as he passed the picture over to Catelyn and Daniel. "Is there anyone from the home or where you worked before you moved here that would be mad at you about something? Could someone have followed you here?"

Her mouth worked and she gulped. "Um. No. Not that I know of. I mean I generally just kept to myself." She flushed. "It's hard to make friends with a big old chip on your shoulder." Her words came slow as though she was embarrassed to admit it. "Unless…" She bit her lip and looked away.

"What?"

"There was this boy. Bethany's age. He was crazy about her back in North Carolina."

Mason narrowed his eyes. "Let me guess. You weren't crazy about him."

She gave a negative shake of her head. "I thought he was too sophisticated for her. Too mature. Too…everything. I came home early from one work one day and I caught them making out on the couch." Anger glittered in her eyes. "I said a few things I shouldn't have, really laid into both of them, but mostly him." She shrugged. "But we moved here the next week and Bethany hasn't heard from him since."

"That you know of," Mason muttered. Already he wanted to wrap his hands around the young man's throat. His emotion shocked him. Was this what being a father of a teenage girl felt like?

Exchanging a glance with Daniel and Catelyn, Mason asked, "What's his name?"

"Austin Howard."

Catelyn wrote it down. "I'll check this out and get back to you."

Daniel had already bagged the picture. He nodded to the window. "Looks like the window's been jimmied."

Lacey let out another gasp. "Is that how someone got in? Bethany said someone was in her room one night…."

"I would say it's possible."

"All right, let's get that window fixed," Mason intervened as he looked at Catelyn. "While you guys take care of this, Lacey and I will head over to Georgia's house and see if she will be a little more forthcoming now."

Catelyn nodded. "I'm going to get Joseph to do some digging into this Austin Howard fellow and see what he's been up to the last couple of days. I also want to see where he was the night of the car accident."

Nodding his agreement, Daniel wrote something in his notebook and said, "I'll check with the lab and see where they are on the car."

In agreement, they finished up in Bethany's room then split up to go their separate ways.

Mason was still in the processing stage.

He had a daughter. He really did.

He jerked as he realized he had to tell his family—his dad, sister and his stepmother.

Then winced at the thought of how that would go over.

They'd be furious.

Not at the fact that Bethany existed, but at the fact they hadn't been able to spoil her rotten for the past fifteen years. His heart thudded. Not to mention that they'd be crushed if Bethany was gone for good, and they never got to meet her.

His father had remarried almost ten years ago,

although Mason wondered how he found the courage to trust again after what his mother had done. Grudgingly, as the years passed and he watched the two of them together, he had to admit that his stepmother, Maggie, seemed to be perfect for his father.

Mason's sister, Carol, had been married for three years and professed she had neither the time nor the desire to have a child that would interfere with her budding acting career.

Which was one reason why she rarely came home. Carol declared she couldn't stand the subtle comments about her biological clock ticking away and the accompanying sad-eyed looks at her minuscule waist.

He shook his head and almost smiled. Mason would become Carol's favorite person as soon as he produced Bethany to his parents.

Mason's smile turned south.

If he produced her.

His fingers gripped the steering wheel. No, there was no *if* about it. He *would* find her. He had to.

He spun the wheel and pulled onto Georgia's street. Three houses down he parked in front of a brick ranch with a nicely kept yard. A blue Mustang convertible sat in the drive.

Georgia's car.

"She's home." Lacey's soft words slammed

into him. He'd driven the entire way to Georgia's house so consumed by his own thoughts he hadn't opened his mouth to utter a word.

He looked at Lacey. "I'm sorry."

The soft look in her eyes shook him. She still had that uncanny ability to read him when he dropped his guard enough. She knew what he meant by the apology.

Her fingers reached out to loosen his from the steering wheel. The warmth of her hand seared him as she reassured him. "You don't have to explain. You've got a lot to think about." Her gaze swung back to the house. "I want to talk to her this time."

"Lacey…"

Her jaw firmed into a rock that he remembered from their teen years. He might as well keep his arguments to himself. Instead of trying to persuade her to let him do the talking, he simply nodded.

"Fine."

Lacey raised a brow at him when he still made no move to get out of the car. "What is it?"

"What's she like? What's her favorite color? Gold? She had a lot of gold in that room."

Lacey sighed. "Well, when she was thirteen and in the Goth phase, she was really into black."

He winced. "Goth?"

"Uh-huh. But it didn't last long. I just let her

do her thing and didn't say much about it. Even when she came home one afternoon from school with jet-black hair." She shook her head and gave a small smile. "I was horrified, but I didn't say anything except that change wasn't always a bad thing and I'd get used to it."

He gave a small laugh. "What did Bethany say?"

"She was miffed that I didn't blast her and give her the argument she wanted." She cut her eyes at him. "This whole Goth thing was an attempt to get me to tell her your name."

His eyes lost their smile. "Did it work?"

"Almost," she whispered. "But I just couldn't. Not at that time. In spite of having a dad for a preacher, I was a new Christian and was just learning my way. I had to go at my own pace." She sighed. "But I did sit her down and we had a long talk about you."

"Minus the name, of course."

"Yes, minus the name." She looked out the window. "But it seemed to help. After that, she let the dye grow out and stopped wearing black all the time. Now her favorite colors are gold and green."

Mason drew in a deep breath. The more she told him about Bethany, the more he wanted to meet the girl. He just hoped Georgia was the one that was going to make that possible. "Are you ready?" he asked.

"Yes."

Mason opened the door and climbed out of the car. Lacey did the same and they walked side by side up the path to the front door.

Lacey reached out a finger and pressed the doorbell.

The girl he'd just questioned a few hours earlier opened the door with a smile that quickly turned into a frown when she saw him. When her eyes landed on Lacey, the frown tightened into a look of fear. "Ms. Gibson? Have you found Bethany?"

Lacey took the girl's hand and gave her fingers a squeeze. "Not yet, hon. And that's why I really need to talk to you. Is it all right if we come in?"

Georgia licked her lips, looked over her shoulder then back at them. "Um, sure. I guess."

Lacey noticed that fear still lingered in Bethany's friend's gaze. Georgia led them to a nice-sized living area. The white walls and French doors made it seem larger than it actually was. The tan leather couch and matching love seat complemented the room.

"Do I need to get my mom?"

Mason gave her a comforting smile. "Not unless you want to. I'm not here in an official capacity."

He glanced at Lacey. "I'm here to support Bethany's mother, I guess you could say."

"Okay. Well, just let me tell her you're here. I'll be right back."

True to her word, she returned within seconds and said, "Mom said you could talk to me." She sounded like she wished her mother had refused.

Georgia waved them to the sofa while she chose the cushioned rocker on the opposite wall. One bare foot tapped the floor in a silent nervous gesture.

Lacey looked the girl in the eye and leaned forward. "Please, Georgia, tell us what happened the night of the wreck. I know Bethany was there—and you were, too. Please, please, be honest. Right now, you're my only hope of finding Bethany."

Georgia swallowed hard and tears filled her eyes. "Ms. Gibson, I'm sorry…I…"

"Tell the truth, Georgia."

The quiet voice filled the room. Lacey looked to her left to see Georgia's younger brother standing in the connecting door that led to the kitchen. He was about thirteen years old and a male copy of his sister from his dark curls to green eyes.

Georgia's nostrils flared and she blinked rapidly. "Go away, Nate."

Her words lacked force and didn't faze the young man. Shoving his hands into the front pockets of his khaki cargo shorts, Nate stepped toward Georgia. "You were there that night. I saw you slip out and get in the car with Kayla."

Lacey breathed a surprised gasp, and Nate turned toward her. "I think Bethany was in the car that night, too. There was someone else in the passenger side. Could have been her."

"Why didn't you say anything before this?" Lacey asked.

Nate shrugged. "Because Georgia asked me not to. She said she'd get in a ton of trouble for sneaking out and lying about everything." He frowned at his sister. "But she's been so weird since then, and I don't think some things that have happened to her were really accidents. I'm scared for her." He flushed. "I kept quiet because she could get me in trouble for something I did at school, but if she's in some kind of danger…"

Mason looked at Georgia. "So you blackmailed him?"

Georgia jumped up. "I had to! Don't you understand?"

At her shout, Georgia's mother entered the room, her eyes taking in the agitation of her daughter and her guilty-faced son. "What's going on?" She looked hard at Mason and Lacey. "When I said you could talk to Georgia, I didn't mean you could have her in tears."

Lacey bit her lip and stared at Georgia, ignoring

the girl's mother. "No." She kept her voice as neutral as possible. "I don't understand. Could you please explain it to me?"

Mason jumped in with his own question. "What accidents, Georgia?"

Nate answered for his sister. "A car almost ran her off the road a couple of days ago. And then we were at the mall last Saturday with Bethany and someone tried to shove her down the escalator."

"What?" Georgia's mother gasped. "Why didn't you tell me any of this?"

Severely agitated, Georgia looked back and forth between Nate and her mother. Then she let out a groan and sank back onto the chair. "All right," she finally whispered, "I was there the night of the wreck." She looked up. "Bethany was there. We were *all* there."

"Georgia?"

The girl ignored her mother's horrified whisper and shot a look at her brother so full of agony that Lacey gasped. Then Georgia took a deep breath and said, "We all snuck out and Kayla picked up Bethany first, then came after me."

"I knew it," Lacey replied as her heart thudded in her chest. Was she finally going to hear what happened that night?

EIGHT

Mason watched Georgia's face and wondered at the sheer terror washing over it. What had happened to instill such fear in the poor girl? His stomach lurched. What had happened to Bethany? Would he even have the chance to meet his daughter?

He listened as Georgia drew in a shaky breath and continued. "We were supposed to meet up with a couple of guys from school." She swiped a hand across her lips and rolled her eyes toward the ceiling. "But we never got there. Bethany and Kayla were in the front. Kayla got a text message and started to answer it, and Bethany yelled at her to quit texting and to pay attention to the road."

"Texting?" Mason's gut clenched and anger flowed through him. Would people never learn? Not just teens, but adults, too. Driving and texting was a deadly combination.

"Kayla." Georgia laughed without humor. "Well, you couldn't tell her anything. She just kept on answering the text. Bethany grabbed for the phone and Kayla shoved her away. Bethany refused to speak to her while Kayla was texting and the next thing I know, we're wrapped around a tree."

She shook her head. "We were all pretty stunned. But I managed to open my door and get out. I remember Bethany screaming Kayla's name and then—nothing. I think I passed out. When I woke up it couldn't have much later. Maybe a couple of minutes because Bethany was still trying to get Kayla to wake up." She swallowed hard and choked out, "Only she wouldn't."

Georgia's mother walked over and took the girl's hand. Georgia shook her off and swiped at her eyes. "And then *he* was there."

"Who?" Mason's adrenaline flowed through his veins as though he were facing down a fugitive who had the upper hand.

"I don't know. I've never seen him before. Or since."

"What did he do? Did he want to help?"

"I thought so at first and Bethany seemed to know him because she said something like, 'I'm so glad you're here,' but then he grabbed Bethany and tried to get her to come with him. When she wouldn't leave us behind—" Georgia gulped "—he pulled out a gun."

"What?" Lacey placed a hand over her mouth

and stared wide-eyed at Georgia who nodded and closed her eyes. Georgia's mother looked ready to pass out. When Georgia opened her eyes, she looked at Lacey. "I'm so sorry. I wanted to tell you but…" She bit her lip.

"But what? You have to tell what you know, Georgia," the girl's mother demanded.

Georgia shot her mother an irritated look and continued. "He grabbed her and started dragging her to his car. She was screaming and fighting him, trying to use her karate on him. She got loose from him, but he did something that tripped her. She fell, and he grabbed her again. I found a tree branch that had fallen off and hit him in the head with it. He let go of Bethany and dropped the gun. It went off and a bullet hit him in the leg, I think, because he fell on the ground. Bethany screamed at me to run. I did, but not before I heard him yell at her."

"What did he yell?" Mason asked.

After another hard swallow, she croaked, "'This isn't over! I'll find you! Go to the cops or tell anyone about this and your mom is dead! You hear me? She's dead!'"

"He threatened me?" Lacey squeaked. "That's why Bethany wouldn't talk to me?"

Georgia gave a slow nod, and Mason's heart nearly broke for the daughter he'd yet to meet. How scared she must be. He had to find her—desperate to hold her and tell her everything would be all right.

Please, God…

The prayer slipped through his mind and for the first time in a long time he didn't push it away. He wanted to bargain with God. If God would do something to help Bethany, Mason would swallow his pride and relinquish his long-held anger against the God who hadn't done anything to stop his mother from walking out on her family. Shame hit him. He knew God didn't work that way.

Reining those thoughts in, he looked at Georgia. "And that's why you didn't say anything?"

"Partly. But also because…" She broke off and sighed. "I'll be right back."

She slipped from the room and disappeared down the hall. When she returned, she carried a piece of paper. Mason took it from her and read aloud. "'Tell anyone what you saw that night and your brother, Nate, will be next.'"

A harsh gasp from Georgia's mother sent Lacey to the woman's side. Mason watched her offer comfort even while his mind clicked with questions. "Georgia, when did all the weird things start happening with you and Bethany?"

Georgia raised a hand to rub her forehead. "Um…about a month ago, I guess. And it wasn't every day. Just every once in a while. Out of the blue, something weird would happen. Then it would be quiet for a couple of days. Then something else…you get the idea."

Mason did a quick calculation. "The car wreck happened during spring break. That was the beginning of April. We're now halfway through the month of June—about ten weeks later."

Lacey frowned at him. "Right."

"The incidents started about a month ago. Why wait so long after the car accident to make another attempt to grab Bethany or come after you? He knew you saw him, right?"

"Yes." Georgia gave a slow nod.

Mason looked at Lacey and saw Georgia's confusion mirrored in her eyes. He said, "He was recovering. Georgia said she thinks he got hit by the bullet."

The light went on for Lacey and she jumped in. "So that's why everything was quiet after the wreck. He was hiding out. Once he recovered, he must have realized his threat worked, when there was no report of an attempted kidnapping and Georgia and Bethany weren't named in the news in relation to the wreck. Which left him free to try again," she responded.

"Exactly."

"Then how do we go about tracking this person down?" Lacey demanded.

Mason looked at Georgia. "You said you think she knew him. Do you know from where?"

"No. She didn't say his name or anything. And I've never seen him."

Mason rubbed a hand across his head. "All right. Here's what you can do to help a little more. I know it's been a while, but we need you to work with a sketch artist."

The teen gulped but nodded. "O-okay. And, um, now that you know pretty much everything, you should probably also know that Bethany called me a couple of hours ago."

From her position next to Georgia's mother, Lacey bolted to attention and zeroed in on the girl. "She *called* you? Why didn't you tell me right away?"

Georgia's gaze flicked from one adult to the next. "Because I wasn't going to say anything at all about anything. But—" she bit her lip "—I think she's in some really big trouble and needs help in spite of the fact that she didn't want Ms. Gibson knowing about the threat. She was going to deal with it her own way."

"How did she think she was going to do that?" Mason demanded.

Georgia shrugged. "She said she was going to find her dad and he would help her."

Mason winced and shared a look with Lacey. Her heart thudded. "I don't know how she planned to find him. She doesn't have any idea who he is."

"Yeah, she does. At least she thinks so." Georgia looked Lacey in the eye. "She found your diary in an old box when you moved and started reading it."

Lacey felt the air leave her lungs as though the words had physically punched her in the stomach. Her diary? *Oh, Lord,* she prayed, *not that.* "But I never mentioned his name in the diary. I only used initials."

"Oh." Georgia looked doubtful. "Well, all I know is Bethany said she was going to talk to everyone in the city whose initials were MGS. She was going through the phone book one by one."

Lacey glanced at Mason. Poor Bethany. She never would have found him. His number was unlisted. Lacey had had to get it from her mother who got if from his stepmother under false pretenses. For once, her mother had done something to really help her out. It had been the start of the reparation of their relationship.

Mason rubbed a hand across his eyes, then said, "Georgia, I need your phone number. I'm going to see if I can get Bethany's call traced."

She rattled it off for him and he got on his cell phone to pass the number on to one of his contacts at the police station. Probably Joseph or Catelyn. Or Daniel.

After Mason hung up, he said to Georgia, "Okay, now I need your cell phone."

"What?" The teen looked at him like he'd sprouted another head.

"If Bethany calls again, I want to be the one to answer."

With a huff of disgust, she dug her phone out of her backpack and handed it over. "She's going to be really mad at me about this."

"As long as she's alive to be mad, I'll take it," Lacey muttered.

They exited Georgia's house and climbed back into the car.

By this time, the sun was disappearing on the horizon and Lacey's stomach growled its hunger.

Mason glanced at her as he stuck the key into the ignition. "Hungry?"

She placed a hand over her middle and flushed. "You heard?"

"I'd have to be deaf not to."

A giggle escaped her before she could stop it. Then sadness immediately engulfed her. He could always make her laugh. Even in the worst of times. Times like now. A time when she had no right to feel the slightest bit of levity.

She blinked when he leaned over and pulled her into a light hug. Stunned, she froze. What was he doing? Why was he trying to offer her comfort when she'd kept his daughter from him?

He must have felt her tension, the confusion

emanating from her, because he let her go and started the car without another comment.

But she still felt his arms around her. Still smelled his spicy cologne. The same cologne he used sixteen years ago.

"I'm sorry," she blurted.

He glanced at her as he pulled away from the curb. "For?"

"Keeping Bethany away from you. Regardless of how we parted, I should have found a way to tell you. To make you listen." It was hard to swallow her pride and admit that. Yes, he'd been wrong, too, but once she'd worked through the hurt and come to know Christ, she should have contacted him.

But she hadn't.

"I'm sorry about that, too."

"No matter what you believe, I didn't cheat on you with Daniel." She sucked in a deep breath and waited for his response.

Disappointment sliced through her when he didn't give her one. Instead, he pulled into the parking lot of the local fifties-style restaurant where customers ordered and ate in the car.

It was late and there was only one other car in the parking lot. A cute waitress, probably working her way through college, approached the vehicle. Lacey gave her order and then Mason did the same.

Then silence settled over them. An uncomfortable one that made her want to squirm. She refused.

Finally, he broke the quiet. "I want to believe you, Lacey. I just…" He stopped and drew in a deep breath. "I can't believe this is happening sixteen years later. Seeing you again has brought back all kinds of feelings I thought I'd…" Once again he paused. "Bethany sounds like a great kid. You've done a good job with her."

"She likes to paint," Lacey blurted.

He jerked. "What?"

"You remember how you'd always bring your sketch book to the lake and draw anything that caught your attention?"

A soft smile curved his lips. "Yeah."

"Bethany loves to paint. Oil, watercolor, whatever."

"The beach scene in your living room?"

She nodded. "Bethany did it about two years ago."

A low whistle filled the car. "Wow, she's good."

"I know. I tried to get her to take some serious art classes, but she said she wanted to focus on the karate." Lacey shrugged. "So I let her. I certainly wasn't going to force her to paint if she didn't want to."

A finger reached out and traced her ear. She

shivered and locked her eyes on his. He leaned toward her. "I've missed you."

His words pulverized her heart. How she'd longed to hear him say that. She'd missed him so much. Lacey leaned in to him, wanting to be in his arms and have him tell her everything was going to be okay. That they could forget the past and move forward into the future together. That everything bad they'd experienced didn't matter.

But he still believed Daniel's lies about her.

She pulled back.

But it did matter. And the past was bulldozing it's way right into the present. "Mason, I want to…"

The back windshield shattered and Lacey screamed as Mason grabbed her left arm and yanked her down.

NINE

Mason felt the car shudder. Lacey's scream echoed in his ears. "Stay down and call 9-1-1!"

He grabbed the handle and flung the door open, rolling to the ground and reaching for the weapon he'd strapped on early that morning. He winced at the pull in his still-healing shoulder but ignored it.

His eyes scanned the parking lot and he noticed the other car's occupant on the phone. He wanted to yell at the man to get his head down. Instead, he searched for the shooter.

"Mason!"

Lacey's shout warned him.

He whirled to see a figure dart through the trees toward the back of the parking lot. Mason bolted after him. "Freeze! U.S. Marshal!"

Of course the figure kept going.

And so did Mason.

Through the parking lot, dodging the employees craning to see what's going on. "Get back inside!"

They scrambled to do so, understanding the seriousness of what was happening. Mason pushed himself faster, desperate to catch the person who could possibly lead him to his daughter.

The man, dressed in dark jeans, a black T-shirt and a baseball cap, skirted a Dumpster and headed past another alley. Mason stayed on him, thinking he ran pretty well for someone with a limp. But Mason was gaining on him.

He followed him across a four-lane road and into another stand of trees.

Almost there. Mason felt his satisfaction surge as he closed in, reached out to snag the man's shirt—and felt his foot hook under an exposed root.

He landed on the rough ground with a grunt and felt fire shoot through his left shoulder.

The pain stunned him for only a second, but by the time he bolted to his feet, the man was gone. Tromping in the direction the suspect had fled, he looked to the right, then the left.

Nothing.

Mason pulled up and bent double, hands on his knees. Again, his eyes swept up one side of the street then down the other.

Where had he gone?

Buildings lined the street. Cars passed him. Normality surrounded him.

And his daughter was still lost.

Mason pounded his fist against his thigh and let out a growl of frustration. Then the normality changed. Lights flashed, sirens sounded. He gave the area one more scan and realized it was hopeless.

The man had disappeared.

Either into a waiting car or one of the buildings lining the street. There was no way to know. No way to effectively search each and every place on his own.

With one last look over his now-aching shoulder, he swiped at the sweat dripping from his temples and made his way back to the restaurant parking lot. Catelyn, Joseph and Daniel already worked the scene.

Lacey stood off to the side looking pale and shaky. Scared, but determined. He went straight to her and grasped her upper arms. She folded into him and he held her against his chest expecting her to break into sobs.

She didn't.

But she did let him hold her. And holding her brought memories. Memories of fun times, memories of thinking he'd be with her forever.

And then the memory of finding her in Daniel's arms.

A memory she claimed was false.

A memory he'd not let her explain, because if he let her and then couldn't believe her…

He swallowed hard and set her back away from him. "I'm sorry. I couldn't catch him."

She nodded and looked toward Catelyn and Joseph. "Have they found anything?"

"Let me check."

Mason made his way over to Catelyn, avoiding Daniel's penetrating gaze.

The man hadn't missed the embrace.

With gloved hands, Catelyn held up a concrete block the size of a two by four. Mason raised a brow. "So, it wasn't a bullet."

"Nope, but if that had hit one of you, it might have felt like one."

Lacey rubbed her arms as if chilled in the eighty-five-degree heat. "What was the purpose of that?" she asked, bewilderment stamped on her drawn features. "That's not going to kill anyone, so why bother with the petty vandalism?"

"And take a chance on getting caught," Mason agreed. He shook his head. "I don't know. You're right, it doesn't make any sense."

Catelyn nodded toward the concrete block. "I don't think we'll find any prints on this, but I'll have the lab look at it anyway. Maybe we'll get lucky."

Mason had a feeling she was right. There'd be no fingerprints on it. The person doing this wasn't stupid. There had to be a motive. But what?

"Did you get a look at the guy?" Daniel asked.

"No." Mason blew out a disgusted sigh. "He had on a baseball cap, a black T-shirt and black pants that could have been jeans. He took off through the woods, which were pretty dark. But he was limping like he had a bum leg."

"Which would fit with what we know about the man who tried to kidnap Bethany the night of the wreck," Lacey offered.

Daniel nodded, and Lacey edged closer to Mason, her eyes darting toward the woods then back to the street. Her anxiety and fear cut through his heart.

"What now?" she whispered.

Mason led her to the damaged car. The air conditioner wouldn't do much against the night heat pulsing around them and through the broken window, but at least it was a ride. "We get you home where you can get some rest then start all over tomorrow."

What he didn't tell her is that he planned to keep working tonight. He had a few ideas he wanted to check out and would do that while she slept.

Although, if the way she was looking at him—as

if he were crazy—meant anything, his plan might be in for a big revision.

"Rest?" she sputtered. "In the house that Bethany is still missing from? With someone out there who seems to be watching us?" She gave an unladylike snort. "I don't think so." Narrowing her gaze at him and crossing her arms across her chest, she demanded, "What's our next move?"

Admiration for her welled up inside him, surprising him with the intensity of his emotions. Her baby was missing, and she wasn't stopping until the girl was found.

And neither was he.

"I think we should check the hospitals for anyone who came in with a gunshot wound the night of the wreck."

"You think he actually would have shown up in a hospital?" Doubt clouded her eyes.

He shrugged. "It's possible and definitely worth checking out."

Lacey nodded and slid into the passenger seat of the car.

"Wait a minute," she called as she jumped from the vehicle.

Mason and Catelyn turned.

"He limped," Lacey blurted.

"Who? The guy I just chased? I know."

Lacey waved her hand. "No, no. The guy that attacked me outside the print shop."

Catelyn lifted a brow. "Really?"

"You didn't tell us that," Mason observed.

"I didn't remember until now. But his shadow at the door—he walked back and forth and I remember thinking he moved funny. Then after he shoved me, I turned enough to catch a glimpse of him running away. He limped."

Catelyn turned to Mason. "You think this was the same person?"

He lifted his almost-healed shoulder and winced. He hoped he hadn't reinjured it too much. "It's hard to say, but I almost wouldn't doubt it. How many men with limps are coming after us?"

"All right," Catelyn said. "I'm going to go get this report written. I'll be in touch."

Mason and Catelyn said their goodbyes.

Ten minutes later, Mason pulled up in front of her parents' home. The motion detector porch light flicked on, immediately transporting Mason back to his senior year of high school, when he'd been madly in love with the girl Lacey used to be.

She turned to look at him and he gave her a slow smile. From the light of the moon, he could see a slight flush grace her cheeks. So, he wasn't the only one tripping down memory lane. "We had some good times, didn't we?"

"We did." She stared at him, not moving.

He wondered what she was thinking.

* * *

She should have forced him to listen to her that day. The day she'd gone to him to tell him of the pregnancy. The day he'd implied she had no morals whatsoever. The day he'd crushed her spirit and sent her running home to throw various items into a suitcase, finally giving in to her parents' demands that she move to a home for unwed mothers.

Her father, now a retired pastor, had been mortified that his only daughter had come home pregnant. There'd been no way the congregation could find out about that. So they'd shipped her off.

It had been the best thing that could have happened to her, although she sure hadn't thought so at the time.

"I'm not like your mother, Mason."

He flinched and looked away from her.

"I'm sorry. I probably shouldn't have blurted that out." She wrapped her fingers around the door handle ready to bolt from the vehicle when Mason's warm hand stopped her.

"I was wrong that day," he admitted with a frown, as though pushing the words past his lips was done with great effort. "I shouldn't have said what I did, called you those names…."

"Don't…"

"No," he said, shushing her. "I owe you an apology." Swallowing hard, he looked away. "When you came to me that day, all I could see was you kissing Daniel."

"I wasn't kissing him! He was kissing me. He set us up! Can't you see that?"

Mason finally met her eyes. "He said you came on to him, that you grabbed him and kissed him. He was my best friend, Lacey. Why would he say that?"

He still doubted her. The pain she'd felt sixteen years earlier returned full force. "It doesn't matter now. Just—let's forget about the past and focus on the present. Finding Bethany is all that matters right now."

TEN

He took her hand. "Can we sit in the sunroom for a few minutes? The blinds are drawn and it's probably safe."

"Why?" she whispered, still feeling the course of pain running through her, brought on by old memories.

"I want to know more about Bethany."

How could she refuse? He looked eager—and scared, and hopeful all at the same time. With a sigh, she pulled out her keys and nodded. "Sure." She unlocked the door and motioned to the two-seater swing. Settling herself on it, she waited. He hesitated for a brief moment and sat beside her.

Swatting a mosquito away from his nose, he asked, "It's not too muggy for you?"

She got up, walked to the air-conditioning window unit and flipped it on. Cool air rushed out. "That'll help."

He drew in a deep breath. "Are your parents home?"

"Yes. They're sitting by the phone desperately praying for it to ring."

"Have you told them everything?"

She sighed. "Not everything. Although I have warned them to be extra careful. Bethany wouldn't leave on her own. And I think the incidents that have happened have proved that." She paused when he leaned closer, his breath tickling the hair above her right brow.

Her heart stuttered at the look in his eyes. And yet she wanted throw up a protective barrier around her emotions. When she was around him, she felt like she was on a roller coaster without a safety harness.

And she couldn't work up the energy to be angry at him. She could tell he was on the same ride.

"I agree." His hand came up to cup her chin. "You haven't changed a bit, Lacey."

Lacey jerked, but his fingers tightened and she stilled. Then she gave a short laugh. "Oh, yes I have, Mason."

He winced. "I didn't mean that in a derogatory way. I meant—" he drew in a deep breath "—seeing you again has brought back all kinds of feelings I'm not sure what to do with."

His honesty surprised her. And endeared him to her. "I can appreciate that, Mason."

Mason leaned back and blew out a sigh. He

changed the subject. "And your parents don't have any suggestions as to what might have happened to Bethany?"

"No, I've already told you that. I know for a fact that she wouldn't have left on her own. Other than that, I'm clueless."

"I agree with you, but what makes you so 100 percent sure?"

She had to tell him. "Bethany will be furious with me for telling you this, but…" She bit her lip.

He frowned. "What?"

"She's a big chicken."

"Chicken?" He blinked. "As in scared?"

Lacey felt an amused smile cross her lips as she thought about her daughter. "Yes. Growing up, Bethany never even spent the night at a friend's house. For some reason, she's always been fearful of being away from me at night. Even at the 'mature' age of fifteen, she hates spending the night away. All of her sleepovers are usually under my roof."

He nodded. "Okay, I can see why you're so convinced she didn't run away. And after what Georgia told us about someone trying to kidnap Bethany the night of the wreck…" He blew out a sigh. "I'm afraid that whoever was after her that night may have finally caught up with her."

Lacey felt her heart plummet, although he

hadn't voice anything she hadn't already thought. "I know."

His arms came around her and this time she let him hold her.

"This feels right, Lacey," he whispered into her ear.

She shivered. It did feel right. But the timing…

The door opened and Lacey pulled away from Mason to settle back against her side of the swing.

Her mother stepped out into the sunroom. "I thought I heard voices." Her eyes landed on Mason and grew wide. "Mason Stone?"

"Yes, ma'am." He sounded hesitant as though not sure of his welcome.

Lacey watched a warm light come into her mother's eyes. "Well don't just sit there, come on in."

Relief filled Lacey. Her mother's reaction to Mason's presence told her that the past was well and truly forgotten. Or, if not forgotten, at least forgiven.

By her mother anyway.

Mason's forgiveness was still another story.

Lacey always suspected that her mother hadn't agreed with her father's decision to send Lacey to the home for pregnant girls, but the woman hadn't had the guts to stand up to him.

It hadn't taken long to see how her father had mellowed with age.

And retirement.

She supposed it didn't matter what his former congregation thought about him now. From the casseroles and baked goods she'd seen lining the kitchen countertops this morning, the people of the church were bound and determined to take good care of their former pastor and his prodigal daughter.

Once inside, Mason filled the room and Lacey shivered at the reality of him back in her childhood home. He'd been a frequent visitor before she'd found out she was pregnant...and before Daniel had driven them apart.

Mason's phone rang as her mother led them into the kitchen. He stepped back outside to talk, and Lacey's mother zeroed in on her. "We'll talk about Mason later. For now—nothing about Bethany?"

Lacey shook her head as she took a seat at the kitchen table. "We're waiting to hear from the lab about some DNA and some other stuff, but so far nothing."

"She didn't just take off, did she?" Real fear colored her mother's eyes for the first time since learning of Bethany's disappearance.

"No, Mom, I'm afraid not."

Lacey debated about whether or not to tell her

mother the details of the day. Before she had time to make a decision, Mason returned, a grim look on his face.

"We have a fingerprint from the car."

Lacey raised a brow. "Already?"

Mason gave her a humorless smile. "I have friends in high places."

"So who does it belong to?"

"We don't know. He's not in the system."

Lacey felt her shoulders sag. "Then what good is the print?"

"Because we have something to match up to any suspects we might come up with. The print doesn't match any of the girls' or the girls' list of friends Daniel got from Kayla's mother. My hope is that it's going to be a match to our guy with the limp."

"If you can catch him."

Mason nodded. "I'll catch him."

Lacey's mother waved him to the seat opposite Lacey and he sat. She placed a fresh cup of coffee in front of him and handed him the sugar.

With a start, Lacey realized her mother remembered how he took his coffee. The pleased look on Mason's face said he was thinking the same thing.

While Mason stirred in his sugar, Lacey bit her lip, then asked softly, "Do you want to see her baby album?"

Mason looked at her. "More than anything."

Lacey's mother bustled from the kitchen saying, "I'll get it."

Within a minute, she returned with the thick book. She handed it to Lacey and said, "I'll just be in the den with your dad. Let me know if you need anything."

Shooting a warm smile at her mother, Lacey opened the cover and Bethany's very first picture stared back at them. "That was when I was twenty-four weeks along. It's an ultrasound. That's the day they told me she was a girl."

Mason reached out a finger and traced the image, his expression one of awe.

She turned the page. "This is her when she was a couple of days old. She was so tiny." Lacey thought back to the day she'd brought Bethany home from the hospital. "Home" as in her rented room at the boarding house.

"It was hard, wasn't it?" Mason asked, his shrewd gaze taking in the details not only in the pictures, but in her face, too.

She swallowed. "Yes. It was very hard. But the home I stayed in while I was pregnant was very good. They spent a lot of time counseling us, educating us on parenting and what to do when we felt like we were at our wit's end. They also provided a way to get my degree in graphic design. It wasn't where I wanted to be, but I've come to realize it's where I needed to be. So…" She shrugged. "I put a lot of that to good use."

"I'm impressed."

She gave a little laugh. "Well, like I said, it was one of the hardest times in my life." Drawing in a breath, she shook her head. "But I got through it. I look back now and realize it had to be God looking out for me, putting people in my path that I didn't even know I needed, but—" she swiped at a tear that escaped "—we survived and even had a good life there in North Carolina."

"But then it was time to come home."

"Yes." She smiled. "God can be very convincing when it comes to putting wrongs to right, you know?"

Mason pursed his lips. "Yeah. I know." He flipped through each and every page, lingering, studying, learning about his child. When he lifted his eyes, she saw the tears there.

He blinked and the tears dissolved. "Thank you for sharing this with me. It's hard knowing what I missed, but—" he nodded and tapped the album with a finger "—this helps."

Throat tight once again, she nodded. He stood as her mother came back into the kitchen. Looking at Lacey's mother, he said, "Y'all try to get some rest." To Lacey he said, "We'll get back to it first thing in the morning."

"What about the hospitals?"

"I'll let you know if I find out anything, I promise."

Lacey hesitated, fatigue sweeping over her. Yet the thought of Bethany out there, scared, alone…or worse—not alone—made her tremble. "How can I sleep?" she whispered, agony flowing through every part of her.

Mason pulled her into a hug, almost as though he couldn't stop himself and she let herself fold against him. Then she heard him say, "You have to. For Bethany. When we find her, she's going to need you strong and able to care for her."

In her mind, she knew he was right. Convincing her heart wasn't going to be that easy.

Climbing into his car and leaving Lacey behind in her current state of angst wrenched his gut. Almost angry at himself for letting the woman he once considered a cheat of the worst kind weave herself back into his heart within the span of twelve hours, he ordered himself to be wary.

Lacey adamantly denied kissing Daniel, placing all the blame on his friend.

But his mother had very convincingly done the same thing to Mason's father.

Over and over again.

Until she finally just left.

He felt his muscles tense. All his life he'd sworn never to be like his father. To learn from his father's mistakes. Never to fall for a woman's charming lies.

And then he'd met Lacey and fallen hard.

And she'd turned out to be just like his mother.

At least he'd sure thought so at the time.

Now? Doubt beat with an insistent knock on the door to his emotions.

Pulling in a deep breath, Mason drove down Main Street, eyes probing the darkness, desperately hoping to catch a glimpse of a reddish-blond head.

Nothing. There weren't even that many people on the street at this time of night.

As he scanned each and every face he could see, he debated the best way to put his skills to use in order to find Bethany.

One question nagged at him. Why hadn't she simply gone to the cops?

The only answer he could come up with was that Bethany felt as if she couldn't go to the police because, for some reason, she didn't trust them to keep her mother safe.

That bothered him.

Picking up his cell phone, he dialed Joseph's number.

"Hello?"

"Joseph, this is Mason. Sorry it's so late, but I need your FBI connections again."

Mason gave the man the courtesy apology, but he knew the late hour wouldn't bother Joseph, he was used to working when he had to.

"Absolutely. What can I do for you?" Joseph asked.

"I need to know if there were any gunshot-wound treatments at hospitals within a thirty-mile radius of the accident. Specifically males shot in the leg. If so, I need a name and address of each one."

All business, Joseph said, "Give me the details."

Mason provided the date and time of the accident.

"I should know something soon," Joseph promised. "And listen, I was just getting ready to call you, anyway. Bethany called her friend from a pay phone near the homeless shelter. I've got uniforms driving by more often and keeping an eye on the place just in case Bethany shows back up."

"She's not there now?"

"Nope. I already checked. And I'm sending you a picture of the guy the sketch artist came up with according to Georgia's description."

"All right. Thanks."

"One more thing. Austin Howard."

Mason felt his blood start to boil at the mention of the name. "What about him?"

"He's—gone."

Alarms sounded in his head. "Gone? Gone where? And since when?"

"For about a week. His mother said he took off with a group of friends and she hasn't seen him since."

A cold knot settled in the pit of Mason's stomach. "Did she say where they were headed?"

"South. She said the last she heard he was going to find an old girlfriend and they were going to hang in Florida for the rest of the summer."

"Old girlfriend, huh?" He really didn't like the way this sounded. "Did you get the name of the girlfriend?"

"The mother said she wasn't sure. But get this—he's nineteen."

His boiling blood just spilled over into a raging fury. "And he was messing around with a fifteen-year-old?"

Joseph coughed. "It's not his first time. He has a record."

"For?"

"Statutory rape."

Silence settled between them. Then Mason growled, "I hope you have someone in Florida looking for this guy."

"You know I do. I've also got a BOLO on him around town here, too. Apparently, he can be quite a nasty person. His mother said she had to call the cops on him when he was thirteen. He threatened to kill her because she wouldn't let him go out with friends."

"Send me his picture. I want to flash his face to everyone I come into contact with. If this is the guy that snatched Bethany…"

"All right, it's headed your way."

In less than a minute, a good-looking young man appeared on Mason's phone. "Got it."

He hung up and headed for the homeless shelter. Even though Joseph had said she wasn't there, Mason couldn't stop himself from looking. Two blocks later, he cruised past it, eyeing two men on the corner sharing a cigarette.

Had Bethany been staying there?

He swallowed hard as he thought about his daughter staying in a shelter, his heart thudding with the knowledge that she'd been involved with someone like Austin Howard.

God? I know we haven't talked in a while, but she's just a kid. Please protect her.

All of the things he'd seen in his career in law enforcement played through his mind like a bad movie. Sometimes missing teenagers came home. Sometimes they didn't.

Most often they didn't.

Had Austin found her and grabbed her? But the print on the car didn't match anyone in the system. And Austin was in the system.

He sighed and pulled over to the curb to watch the shelter. Picking up his phone, he scrolled through his contacts until he found his father's number.

To call or to wait?

He dialed the number.

"Hello?"

"Hi, Dad, it's me."

His father's gruff voice came through the line. "Been a while since I heard from you. You doing all right? The shoulder okay?"

Mason went along with the small talk for a few minutes, then said, "I have something I need to tell you."

Silence.

"You remember Lacey Gibson. From high school?"

"Yeah, she was that little girl that did a number on you. I remember her."

Mason flinched at the hardness in his father's tone, but didn't address it. His father may have found God, but he still had his rough edges. He sighed. "Dad, Lacey had a baby fifteen years ago. My baby."

A swift drawn-in breath and more silence. Then his father cleared his throat. "Come again?"

"You heard me. Lacey had a daughter. Her name is Bethany."

"I'm a grandfather? You're sure?"

"When you see her picture, you'll know."

"Well then, when do we get to meet her?"

"I need you to—um—ask for prayer for her. Maybe at your church or something. You know I'm not into the whole God thing anymore." However, it seemed he found himself turning to God more and more. Interesting. "She's missing."

"What?" Confusion echoed in Mason's ear. "What do you mean, missing?"

"I'm sorry, Dad. It's a long story, but the basics are Bethany was kidnapped a few days ago, which is why Lacey came to me. She needed my help to find her. It's what I've been working on ever since."

He heard his father talking to someone in the background. Then, "Maggie says you'd better find that girl, she wants to meet her."

"I do, too, Dad. I do, too."

"We'll be praying."

"Thanks. I'll call you when I know anything."

He hung up and stared back at the shelter, the lights turned low and everyone settling in for the night.

His father had met Maggie at a church function and the woman had had a major influence on the man. He'd stopped his workaholic tendencies and had finally shown interest in another woman. It had shocked Mason, but he was glad his dad wasn't lonely. And Maggie was a good woman.

Kind of like Lacey.

Giving up the search for Bethany for now, Mason turned his car toward home.

The dark empty house greeted him and for the first time in a long while he thought about what it would be like to have someone to come home to.

No, not just someone.

Lacey.

His gut tightened at the thought, at imagining her with his ring on her finger. She'd greet him with a hug and a kiss and…

Okay, time to turn his thoughts elsewhere. He'd seen her for the first time after sixteen years and already his imagination was running away from him.

His iPhone buzzed, and he tapped the screen to look at the next picture Joseph had sent him. The sketch.

A dark-haired man with a square jaw, wide-set eyes and thin lips. Not the monster Mason had been expecting. For some reason the mild-looking man surprised him.

He sighed, committed the picture to his memory with a side note to himself that the actual person might not look anything like the sketch.

Pulling out Georgia's cell phone, Mason looked at the number his daughter had called from. A pay phone near the homeless shelter.

It would be one of the first places he'd check tomorrow morning.

Lacey jerked out of a restless sleep and peered at the clock—3:04 a.m.

What had awakened her?

Once the surprise that she'd actually managed to fall asleep faded, she froze and listened to the stillness.

Nothing. Slowly, her muscles began to relax.

Then she heard something.

Lacey shot straight up in the bed, fingers gripping the comforter, her eyes probing the darkness. There wasn't even a full moon to help light the room. Her breath quickened and her heart began to gallop in her chest.

Was someone there?

Her parents?

Or had Bethany come home?

Did she dare call out?

No, not with all the weird things that had been happening lately.

But it was possible, right? It *could* be Bethany trying to sneak in. Maybe. Maybe not.

Hope, that it was Bethany in the house mingled with terror that it wasn't, curled inside her.

Slipping out from under the covers, Lacey tip-toed to the door then paused.

She needed a weapon.

A glance around the room brought nothing helpful in sight.

Pulling in a steadying breath, she paused, strain-ing her ears for the slightest out-of-place noise.

Nothing.

Had she just imagined that she'd heard some-thing? Was it the wishful thinking that Bethany had come home making her crazy?

Or was it one of her parents moving around?

Only one way to find out.

Heart thumping so loud it almost deafened her, she kept to the shadows and made her way down the hall. Pausing at her parents' bedroom door, she peeked in.

Her dad's familiar soft snores reached her ears. A streak of light from the cracked bathroom door lit a line down her mother's face.

Another light thump made her jump.

Smothering a startled gasp, Lacey silently pulled the door shut.

It wasn't her parents.

Bethany?

Oh, please, dear God, let it be her.

Slowly she turned to the room across the hall. The door was shut.

She'd left it open since Bethany's disappearance.

Eager, yet still cautious, Lacey placed her hand on the doorknob, turned it and pushed the door inward.

And screamed her horror.

ELEVEN

The vibrating cell phone snapped Mason awake.

Confused for the brief second it took him to focus on the phone in his hand, Mason finally realized he'd fallen asleep in the recliner, his fingers wrapped around Georgia's phone. His one connection with his missing daughter.

And now it was ringing.

Snatching it to his ear, he barked, "Hello?"

Silence.

"Bethany, is that you?"

Faint breathing reached his ear.

"Bethany," he tried again, "this is your fa—"

Click.

He looked at the number.

It was different from the phone near the shelter.

Immediately, he called Joseph. The man answered on the second ring. "I'm assuming this is important," he stated without ire, sounding wide awake.

"I think Bethany just called. I have Georgia's phone. When I answered, the person on the other line didn't say anything, but I could hear breathing. I need this number traced and you're the one that can get it done yesterday." Mason rattled off the number.

"I'll call you back as soon as I know something."

Mason hung up the phone only to realize he had a call coming in.

Lacey.

Fear shot through him. Something was wrong if she was calling at this hour of the night. He answered. "Lacey, what's wrong?"

"You're right," she whispered through the line. "I've made someone really mad. Come quickly."

At her trembling almost inaudible words, Mason felt his heart thump wildly in his chest. "I'm on my way over."

Less than five minutes later, he was in his car and speeding across the three-mile distance to her house.

When he pulled into her driveway, he noticed every light in the house blazed.

Lacey heard the car drive up.

Mason. He'd beaten the police.

She flew from the house, leaving her parents still shaken and clutching one another as they whispered prayers for their granddaughter's safety.

Lacey launched herself into Mason's arms not caring about the past, what he thought of her—or what anyone else would think if they saw her actions.

She needed him.

"What is it, Lacey?" His lips touched the top of her head, ruffling her hair with his warm breath. "What happened?"

She couldn't seem to stop the trembling. "Oh, Mason, I think she's dead."

Lacey heard herself wail the words but felt like they came from someone else.

Strong fingers gripped her forearms, and she felt him push her away so he could look down at her. Intense blue eyes bored into hers. "Why do you say that?"

"You have to see," she whispered. "In her room."

Two police cars with lights flashing pulled up, followed by Joseph, Caitlyn and Daniel.

Lacey blinked against the harsh red-and-blue lights even as she registered Daniel's presence.

"What's so urgent this couldn't wait till morning?" He looked tired, bleary—and impatient.

Joseph shot the man a surprised look and Catelyn simply raised a brow. Mason lasered his former friend with a look that produced a flush on Daniel's smooth cheeks. "Uh, sorry. It's been a rough night all around." In a more congenial tone, he asked, "What happened, Lacey?"

"Someone was in my house and left another message." Tears trickled down her cheeks. She honestly didn't know how much more of this she could take. *God, why is this happening?*

"What!" Mason exclaimed over her silent, anguished prayer. "Where?"

"Bethany's room." A welcome numbness seemed to come out of nowhere and seep into her bones as Mason let her go to head into the house.

The others followed while Catelyn issued orders into her phone requesting a crime-scene unit.

From the far reaches of her brain, Lacey heard someone caution the others about disturbing a crime scene.

She squelched a hysterical giggle. Her whole house was considered a crime scene. How surreal.

Yet Bethany's continued absence was very, very real.

The thought allowed her to gather her composure and even though she vaguely remembered someone telling her to stay put, she followed, anyway.

Maybe she'd dreamed the scene in Bethany's room.

As she turned the corner to walk down the hall, she heard Mason exclaim and Catelyn draw in a shocked breath.

Coming up behind them, Lacey peered around Mason's shoulder and gave a little whimper.

She hadn't dreamed it.

Mason heard Lacey behind him and tore his eyes away from the scene. Too bad he couldn't delete it from his memory.

Someone had fashioned a white-foam wig stand into a Bethany look-alike, complete with reddish-blond hair, painted blue eyes and a light dusting of freckles across the bridge of the nose and cheeks. Pink lipstick decorated the lips.

But what had him worried was the red liquid someone had place at the base of the neck.

The head had been made to look like it had been decapitated. Crime-scene members worked feverishly throughout the room, a camera flash snapping incessantly.

Mason wrapped an arm around Lacey's shoulders and pulled her to his side. Right now he wasn't thinking about the past, he was racking his brain trying to come up with a reason for everything happening. To Lacey he said, "That's not real. It doesn't mean anything except someone has a twisted desire to see you hurting."

"It could mean…"

He knew what she was trying to say. "No, it doesn't. If someone had really done that to her, they would have left us the real thing. Not…that." He hoped. He caught Joseph's eye. The set of his jaw said he didn't like this one bit. Catelyn consulted with one of the crime-scene techs.

Lacey shuddered, but he felt her shoulders relax a minuscule amount at his reassuring words. "Besides," he confirmed, "I think Bethany called Georgia's phone just a little earlier."

"What?" She jerked to look at him, new hope flaring in her emerald eyes.

"I've got someone tracing the call." He nodded to Joseph. "And Joseph's working on some other things that could help us find Bethany—and who's doing this stuff."

"I'm going to have to move out," she whispered. "I can't stay here and keep my parents in danger."

"No." Mason shook his head. "We need all of you together. Who's to say this person won't go after your parents if they can't get to you?"

As soon as the words left his lips he wished he could take them back. A new fear flashed across her face. Before she could speak, he held up a hand. "We're going to get someone to cover your house—24/7. Right, Catelyn?"

The woman's mouth worked, then snapped shut as her eyes flitted from Mason to the bed to Lacey. "Yes. I think that can be arranged."

"And I've got a couple of buddies I can call if we need some extra help." A light came on in his eyes. "I'll give my partner a call and see what she has on her schedule over the next couple of days. Carly would be glad to help us out." Carly Masterson, soon to be Carly Floyd, would be in the midst of wedding plans. Plans he hated to interrupt, but for Bethany and Lacey, he'd be willing to bet she'd help him out.

Lacey still looked shell-shocked, but didn't protest his offer. Placing a hand on her arm, he pulled her from the room down the hall and into the den where her parents still sat with wide fearful eyes.

Lacey went to her mother and wrapped her in her arms. "It's going to be all right, Mom."

"Why wouldn't you let us go in Bethany's room? What was in there?"

So she'd shielded them, Mason felt his respect for her go up a notch. Come to think of it, it had gone up several notches over the last few hours.

"Someone played a really cruel joke and left a—something that was supposed to resemble Bethany in her room. It freaked me out when I saw it and that's why I screamed." She left out the gruesome details and Mason watched her parents exchange a look that said they knew she wasn't telling them everything. But they accepted her explanation.

Mason spoke into his cell phone, the frown he'd arrived with still creasing his forehead. When he hung up, he turned back to the room's occupants.

Lacey's father rose. "How long are those people going to be here?"

Mason said, "Probably not much longer."

"We're finished," one of the CSU techs said from behind him.

Catelyn and Joseph entered the room, followed by Daniel.

"I'll have someone on the house tonight. We're a little short staffed, so I'm not sure what I can do about tomorrow." He looked at the sky. "Er, today, but I'll talk to the captain and see what he says."

Mason stayed with Lacey and her parents until everyone else cleared out of the house. Once the last car pulled away, he turned to Lacey and said, "The sun's coming up. As soon as Carly gets here, let's find our daughter."

TWELVE

The few hours of sleep she'd managed to get would have to get her through the day.

Not five minutes after Mason asked her what she wanted for breakfast, Joseph called to say he had some news about the gunshot victims dating the night of the accident. He'd narrowed down the list to three men: all had been treated at local hospitals—two the night of the accident, and one the morning after.

Putting off the intention of going to the homeless shelter for later in the day, Mason and Lacey swung through the drive thru. They each consumed a biscuit and the largest coffee sold, while heading to the police station to meet Joseph.

Lacey was quite surprised that Mason wasn't fighting her more on the fact that she insisted on accompanying him everywhere. She absolutely refused to just sit at home and wait for the phone to ring.

That's what her parents were doing and it was close to making them crazy.

Doing her best to focus on the present and on the fact that she was an active participant in the search for Bethany, she stepped inside the police station while Mason held the door for her.

Joseph met them in Catelyn's office. Since he was FBI, he didn't have an official office.

Catelyn wasn't there, but Daniel was.

Great.

Although she had to admit he looked as bleary-eyed as the rest of them. Maybe he was taking Bethany's case more seriously than Lacey had thought.

He got right to it. "We've got three names thanks to Joseph. Mel Simpson, John Howe and Asa Monroe."

Mason shook his head. "Three leg wounds? What are the odds?"

"I can tell you right off that Asa Monroe's not your man. He's sixty-seven years old with a heart condition. His wife got mad because he left his gun on the couch, picked it up and threw it at him. It went off and caught him in the calf."

Lacey winced at the mental picture.

Mason grimaced. "The guy we're after is a lot younger, probably in his late twenties, early thirties. And he was favoring his left leg."

"Then I'm guessing it's John Howe. Shot in the

fleshy part of his thigh. Said he was cleaning his gun when it went off."

"Which leg?" Mason crossed his arms across his chest.

Daniel looked up from the report. "Left."

Lacey asked, "Why couldn't it be the third man?"

"He's dead from an infection caused by the bullet wound."

"Oh."

"So, what do we know about Mr. Howe?" Mason asked.

Daniel studied the file and said, "He's an unemployed truck driver. No previous trouble with the law. Divorced for two years. Has experience in martial arts and is now teaching part-time at the karate school on Brownstock Road." He looked up. "It's also the school Bethany goes to."

A chill raised the hairs on the back of his neck. Mason looked at Joseph. "I'd like to pay Mr. Howe a little visit."

"We need to watch ourselves if this guy tries to pull any of that marital arts stuff on us," Joseph warned.

Mason nodded. "I'm in." He hesitated and looked at Daniel. "Any word on Austin Howard yet?"

The FBI agent hesitated and Mason narrowed his eyes. "What?"

"I wasn't going to say anything yet, but…"

"Just say it, Joseph."

"Austin was spotted in Florida. But he managed to elude capture."

"Capture? Why would he run if he didn't have anything to be worried about?"

Joseph nodded. "Exactly. We're still tracking him down. In the meantime, let's not assume Bethany is with Austin. We have more evidence that she's with a man that limps."

Daniel tossed the file onto Catelyn's desk. "I've got his address, let's go."

Lacey started out the door with the men. Mason hung back and snagged her arm. "You can't go on this visit."

Startled, she looked at him. "Why not? You've let me do everything else with you."

"This is different. We're talking about a guy that might have tried to kidnap Bethany."

She felt the heat of her anger rise up in her. "We're talking about a guy that might have Bethany tied up somewhere in his house. There's no way I'm staying here when Bethany might need me."

Mason set his jaw and Lacey tried not to let him intimidate her. His fingers tightened on her arm, not hard enough to bruise, but hard enough to let her know he was dead serious. "You can't go, understand? It's too dangerous. I promise to be in touch as soon as I know anything."

"But she might…"

Without raising his voice, he said, "The longer we stay here arguing, the longer it's taking us to see if Bethany's there."

"Go," she whispered, knowing she was defeated. "Just go get her."

He pulled her to him for a quick hug and a kiss to her forehead. Looking deep into her eyes, he promised, "I'm going to find her, Lacey. I don't think you coming home is an accident. I think God might have something in mind for us. All three of us."

"God? I thought you didn't…" She broke off again as hope thrummed through her. "Never mind, we'll talk about that later. Go find our daughter."

Without another word, Mason left to catch up with the other two men. Lacey watched him go and felt her heart tumble wildly in her chest.

Hope warred with terrifying fear—hope that they'd find Bethany, and fear that if they did the news wouldn't be good. She began to pace the small office, praying, crying out to God to spare her child and bring her home safe.

Then she thought, what if they did find her? What if they found her and Bethany needed her?

What if she was crying or hurt? Would she wonder why Lacey wasn't there?

She had to go. She had to be there to grab Bethany up in her arms and reassure her that everything was going to be all right.

But where?

She hadn't gotten the address.

And she sure couldn't call Mason and ask him.

Biting her lip, she glanced around the office.

Her eyes landed on the file folder, where Daniel had tossed it.

Crossing to the desk, she took a deep breath, cranked up her nerve and picked it up.

She opened it.

And found the name John Howe.

417 Good Walker Road.

Snatching her phone from her purse, she plugged the address into her GPS. Seven miles from here.

Decision made, she hurried out to the front desk. "I need a cab."

The young officer nodded and placed the call for her. "It should be here within a minute. They tend to hang out around here as we provide them with quite a bit of business."

No doubt.

Hurrying to the front doors, she watched for the yellow vehicle. While she waited, impatiently tapping her foot, another car pulled up and into a parking spot just a few feet away.

Lacey instantly recognized the woman.

Bolting out the door, she hurried over to her. "Janice!"

Her friend jumped and her eyes went wide. "Lacey, what in world is wrong?"

"Can you take me somewhere? I don't have a car and…"

Janice waved her into the passenger seat and started her vehicle. Lacey planted herself into the seat and slammed the door.

"Where are we going?"

Grabbing her phone, she looked at the GPS. "Go left out of here, then take the first right onto Sunbeam Avenue."

Following her directions, Janice spared her a quick glance. "What's going on? Where are we going?"

"To find Bethany's kidnapper."

The car swerved, and Janice shot her another look. "What? Couldn't that be dangerous?"

A pang shot through Lacey. Was she placing the woman in danger? "You don't have to go all the way to the house. I'll get out before you get there and you won't have to worry about anything."

A strange light lit Janice's face and she grinned. "Are you kidding? There's no way you're leaving me out of this. This is the first exciting thing to happen all day." Like an eager kid, she pressed the gas pedal. "Daniel's always the one that gets to be the hero. Maybe this time, I'll get a part in it." Then she cut her eyes to Lacey for a brief second. She reached over with her right and squeezed Lacey's fingers. "I'm sorry. That was really insensitive of me." She placed her hand back on the wheel. "I'm just glad to be able to help you and Bethany."

Lacey didn't know whether to laugh or not. Some things truly didn't change. Janice had never been known for her empathy. Shaking her head, she was just glad Janice was willing to her help her out.

Finally, pay dirt. Nerves stretched taut, Mason's gut clenched as he realized he might very well come face-to-face with his daughter within the next few minutes. He tried not to think about the fact that she might not be alive if he found her. *When* he found her. His mind returned to his impromptu search in the dark last night.

Anxiety twisted inside him and he almost wished he hadn't pushed God aside over the last few years. In fact, saying a prayer to a God who heard him sounded like a really good idea right now. And he hadn't been kidding Lacey when he said he felt as if God might have a plan in bringing her home. He wasn't sure where those words had come from, but they felt right.

Everything that had happened over the last couple of days had thrown him for a loop. And brought him face-to-face with his spiritual side. He would have to explore that whole thing later.

Right now, he had a daughter out there who needed his help. He just prayed he was able to reach her in time.

Mason considered his decision to refuse to allow Lacey to come with them.

But there hadn't been any other option.

This man might very well have their daughter—and a weapon. Mason couldn't concentrate on what he needed to do if he had to watch out for Lacey, too.

She hadn't been happy with him, but her safety was more important than making her happy. Mason watched Daniel drive and wasn't sure whether he trusted the man or not. Right now, he didn't have a choice. "You know we're going to have to talk about the past at some point."

Daniel shot him a look. "Nothing to talk about."

"Come on, Daniel, you know there is."

"I don't think you want to open that can of worms. If there's one thing I've learned over the past few years, it is that dwelling on the past brings nothing but pain and heartache." His fingers clenched the wheel in a death grip. "So just let it go."

Mason wondered what the man meant by that statement and vowed to press deeper when the opportunity presented itself.

Daniel pulled up to a two-story wooden structure that had seen better days, while Joseph pulled in behind them.

The place looked deserted, but experience taught him that didn't always mean it was.

Climbing out of the car, he led the approach to the house at an angle, eyeing the windows, the surrounding properties, every possible place that could harbor a man who didn't want to talk to the police.

Even though the sun shone brightly on the old home, the eerie silence made the hairs on the back of Mason's neck stand straight up. He stopped next to the porch and gripped the railing.

Daniel looked at him and frowned. Mason read the message in the man's eyes. He didn't like it, either.

Long ago, he'd learned to listen to his instincts. Mason reached for the gun secured in the shoulder holster, and let the weighted reassurance rest in his palm.

No sooner had he gripped the butt of the gun, when the door of the house flew open.

A pair of startled brown eyes stared back at him. When John Howe realized who stood on his porch, he spun around and darted back inside.

"Mr. Howe! Stop!"

The uneven receding footsteps told Mason that the man wasn't interested in stopping. And while he hadn't seen a weapon, he kept his gun ready and bolted after the fleeing figure. Joseph had taken off around the side of the house to head Howe off at the back.

Daniel followed after Mason, feet thumping against the dried dirt that looked like it hadn't seen grass or water in a long time.

Rounding the corner, Mason saw Howe execute a martial arts kick to the stomach that landed Joseph on his back gasping for air.

"Freeze, Mr. Howe!" Daniel ordered.

Once again, the man ignored them and with a pained grimace, turned and raced away disappearing back toward the front of the house.

"You okay?" Mason hollered as he raced past Joseph who was scrambling to his feet.

"Just get him," Joseph gritted out through gasps for air.

A screech of brakes and a loud thud reached his ears and coming around to the front of the house he saw a black Mercedes halfway in the driveway.

Mr. Howe lay groaning on the ground in front of the car. "You broke my leg."

As the driver jumped from the vehicle, Mason and Daniel leaped as one to capture the still-stunned John Howe. Daniel slapped a pair of handcuffs on him just as Joseph arrived to stand beside them.

Part of him registered Daniel's wife, Janice, standing with a slack jaw and taking in all the action.

Lacey popped from the passenger seat, hand covering her mouth as she took in the scene. "He just came out of nowhere. Is he all right?"

"My leg," the man groaned.

"What are you doing here?" Mason demanded of her while rolling the man on his side. Without giving Lacey a chance to answer, he glanced at Daniel. "Call the paramedics and some backup." Then he shot a look back at Lacey that he hoped conveyed his anger at her presence, while Daniel stared at Janice, his expression a cross between amusement and anger.

At first Lacey flushed and looked away, then swung her eyes back to his, notching her chin up and setting her jaw.

Daniel shook his head and pulled out his phone to place the calls. Joseph disappeared into the house and Mason knew he was looking for Bethany.

Mason stayed in his crouched position and looked Howe in the eye. He'd have to deal with Lacey later. To Howe, he demanded, "Where's Bethany?"

Howe winced and turned his head away. "She broke my leg, man."

Mason grabbed his shirt and yanked Howe toward him. "I know what's wrong with your leg, Howe, and it's not because you ran into the fender of that car. Now, where's Bethany!"

"I don't know who you're talking about!" Howe's lips curled and Mason wanted to punch him.

"He's talking about my daughter," Lacey suddenly came to life and stomped toward them. "The one you tried to kidnap the night she was involved in a wreck. The wreck where you showed up with a gun." She pointed to his leg. "Which is why you have a bullet wound there. Because you were trying to kidnap my child! Now where is she?"

Her last words ended on a combination of a sob and a scream, and Mason felt his heart clench at her obvious desperation.

A desperation he was beginning to share. Shoving the man in the shoulder, he said, "Look, we've got a witness. Someone who can place you there. You might as well tell us what we want to know."

Howe let out a derisive laugh. "Go ahead and

see if she puts me there. It won't happen because I was never there."

"She?" Mason gave the man a slow smile. "I never said anything about a *she*."

For the first time, uncertainty crossed Howe's face. Then he said, "I heard about that wreck. I figured you were talking about one of those girls that was in it."

"And there was nothing in the news about how many girls were involved." Mason leaned forward. "Keep talking, Howe, you're digging yourself a mighty deep hole. Plus," he said, leaning back and crossing his arms, "we've got blood from the scene. A simple DNA test will tell us if it belongs to you or not."

Mason held his breath. The threat was pure bluff.

"Yeah." Joseph stepped out of the house, looked at Mason and shook his head. Bethany wasn't there. Crushing disappointment hit him hard as Joseph continued to tell Howe, "We've also got a fingerprint we need a match to. I'm sure as soon as we run yours against that, we'll have our answer. Today. Without the DNA testing."

All posturing suddenly left Howe and his shoulders slumped.

An ambulance wheeled in front of the house followed by two police cruisers, lights flashing.

EMTs approached and Mason waved them over, but demanded, "Tell me about Bethany."

Lacey moved closer, desperate to hear every word this man had to say. He knew where Bethany was. He had to. Seeing that their patient wasn't near death's door, the paramedics moved slowly and let the cops ask their questions. They'd done this before.

Mason waited, acting like he had all the time in the world. Joseph crossed his arms and stared the man down. Daniel huddled with one of the other officers.

Howe fidgeted then blurted, "I want my lawyer."

Lacey saw Mason's jaw tighten. That was it then. They couldn't get anything out of him without running the risk of him getting off on some technicality.

"No!" she cried. "Tell me where she is! You taught at the karate school, didn't you? Is that how you know her?"

But the paramedics had already begun their examination of the man's leg and he simply smirked at her.

She wanted to lunge at him and beat him until Bethany's whereabouts burst from him.

But she couldn't.

Mason placed an arm around her shoulders and led her toward the police car.

He leaned in the driver's door and cranked the car, turning the air on full blast. In the backseat of the car, Lacey let the tears fall. She'd been so close. At least it had felt like it. *"Oh, God, help me,"* she cried. *"Help me find my baby, please.*

"Help me," she whispered.

"I'm trying to help you." Mason slid in beside her and all of a sudden the backseat of the sedan felt small. His solid strength filled the area, making her want to lean on it. She didn't bother telling him she hadn't been appealing to him.

"You shouldn't have come here." His voice was tight, his anger tightly leashed.

Swiping the tears with the back of her hands, she turned and narrowed her eyes at him. "I didn't have a choice. The more I thought about the fact that Bethany could be here, that she might be hurt or needing me or…"

She broke off and shrugged, unable to put what was in her mother's heart into words.

His expression softened and he gave a little sigh. "Aw, Lacey, I know, but you can't put yourself in danger like that. You're just lucky that Janice hit Howe. If you'd been standing there when Howe came around the corner of the house, he could have had a weapon, used you for a hostage…" He shuddered and wrapped his arms around her to pull her in for a hug.

He smelled of sweat from the chase and the cologne he'd slapped on this morning, Lacey breathed deep, her heart constricting at the memories the scent evoked. He pulled back. "Did you recognize Howe?"

"No, I've never seen him before. He's definitely not Bethany's instructor. But there are four schools in various locations throughout the city. Maybe he's at a different one than Bethany."

"Joseph said he was a new guy at the one on Brownstock Road. Maybe the whole karate thing is just coincidence."

She sighed. "That's the one Bethany goes to." She threw her hands up. "I don't know. If she couldn't catch a ride with a friend—I just dropped her off at the door and picked her up when she was ready. Her class was right after school and I couldn't take the time off to stay and watch. So—" she shrugged "—I wouldn't know everyone who worked there." Rubbing her eyes to alleviate the headache building there, she asked, "So what now?"

"Now we—"

A rap on the window interrupted him.

Joseph.

Mason opened the door. Joseph leaned in. "Catelyn called. She said the lab got nothing on the two pictures you guys found. They'd been photocopied and the paper was standard, something you can buy anywhere. And no prints except yours."

"Great." Mason nodded and Lacey didn't see any surprise on his face. Joseph had told them exactly what Mason had suspected.

Still, she couldn't help the pang of disappointment. But the fact that Bethany had called Georgia's cell phone reassured her that her child was still alive. Scared and in trouble maybe, but alive. She'd cling to that small thread of reassurance for now.

Daniel and Janice climbed into the front seats. Joseph would follow behind in his car. Mason buckled his seat belt. "What about the cement block he threw in the back windshield of my car? Anything on that?"

"Not yet," Daniel said. Lacey could hear the tightness in his voice. From his body language and the fact that he completely ignored Janice, she could tell he wasn't happy with his wife.

Janice sat silent in the seat, her chin up and her eyes straight ahead.

Mason cleared his throat. "Is he going to the hospital?"

"Yeah, we've got to get him checked out just to cover ourselves. Then we can grill him like a steak when he's released."

Mason blew out a sigh. "Then let's head over

to the homeless shelter. I want to pass Bethany's picture around and see if anyone's seen her."

Finally. Something she could do. She would be in action instead of in this stagnant waiting mode.

"I need to take my wife home," Daniel said.

"But, Daniel, I can help," Janice protested. "Let me hand out pictures. It's the least I can do after all the trouble I caused today." She flicked a glance back at Lacey who felt a guilty flush creep up her throat.

Janice was taking the blame. "Wait a minute, Janice was here because I roped her into helping me. I'm the one you should be mad at."

Mason's fingers curled into fists, attempting to harness his emotions. It was as if Daniel never heard her. He shot a look at Janice and sputtered, "Why would you—" He cut himself off and, with a glance in Lacey's direction, sighed. "Fine."

Daniel drove through the streets of town, and Lacey watched through the window, praying for a sighting of her child. It didn't happen and before she knew it, they'd arrived at the shelter. She grabbed the envelope that contained the flyers and handed one to each of the men and one to Janice.

She couldn't help noticing that Mason studied his a little longer.

When he lifted his eyes, renewed determination glinted.

One by one, they showed Bethany's picture to each person they came in contact with. A few residents stated they'd seen her a couple of days ago.

Lacey saw Janice approach a young woman who shook her head. With a sigh, Lacey walked up to a woman who had a baby on her hip. "Have you seen this girl here?"

The baby gnawed on a knuckle while the woman looked at the picture. "Yeah, I've seen her. She was real nice. Watched Matthew here for a couple of hours one night for me while I got some sleep. I've been sick and she said she didn't mind."

Lacey's heart crimped. "Yes, Bethany loves babies."

"Well, I owe her one. I sure do hope she's all right."

"So do I," Lacey whispered.

Looking up she saw Janice had moved on to a scraggly looking young man. She showed him the picture and he nodded but shrugged as if to say he'd seen her but didn't know where she'd gone.

Mason stood talking to another young woman.

Lacey edged closer to hear the conversation.

"…last night, but something spooked her and she ran off."

"What do you mean, 'spooked' her?" Mason asked the young woman who appeared to be in her late thirties.

She shrugged. "She got a phone call and…"

"Wait a minute," Mason interrupted. "She has a cell phone?"

Impatience flickered across the woman's face. "She did last night. Now do you want to hear this or not?"

"Yes," Lacey interjected. "Please, continue."

"So like I was saying, she got a phone call and this guy starts walking toward her. She sees him and takes off, with him right after her."

Lacey felt some of her hope fade.

"Did he catch her?"

"Nope, she was fast."

"Did the guy chasing her have a limp?"

The woman's brow went up. "Yeah. How'd you know?"

Lacey looked at Mason and saw satisfaction glittering. Then he said, "I've got a lot of questions for Mr. Howe."

THIRTEEN

Mason gave up trying to convince Lacey to go home and get some rest. She was determined to see this through to the end and he didn't blame her. If someone told him he had to stay behind, he would have fought just as hard as she. And because he knew she might pull another stupid stunt like the one where she showed up at John Howe's house, he decided having her close by would be a good thing.

At least he could keep an eye on her.

According to the police officer assigned to him, John Howe would be delivered to an interrogation room in approximately two hours.

He looked at her. "Let's go find a spot to wait."

"All right."

Mason led her down the hallway to the break room. "There's coffee and crackers. Help yourself."

She bit her lip. "Are you sure they won't mind?"

He shot her a smile. "I'm sure."

Lacey grabbed a bottle of water. Mason did the same. They settled on the futon in the corner. Mason studied her, his mind whirling with possibilities. She could have found herself in serious danger today, and, while she'd been upset, she hadn't lost control. He had to hand it to her. When she was determined, she found a way to do what had to be done.

She said, "I know your dad got remarried a few years ago. That's great. So…what are they going to say about all this?"

He shrugged, "I've already told them and they were shocked, of course. Once the idea sunk in, they were thrilled, then terrified for her safety. And sad they missed out on the first fifteen years of her life.

"Maggie, my dad's wife, is a sweet lady. A total opposite of my mother." He swallowed hard. "She doesn't have any children of her own, so she kind of adopted Carol and me even though we were already grown when she and dad married. You'll like her. And if she gets the chance, she'll love Bethany like the grandchild she's been begging for."

Tears filled her eyes and she blinked as she looked away from him. "I'm sorry. I know I was selfish, but I was just so full of hurt and bitterness that I…" She sniffed and Mason felt his heart constrict. "And by the time I finally realized that God didn't hate me, that not everyone in my life would betray me—" she held her hand palm up and gave a tiny shrug "—that was a little over three years ago and I was in my comfort zone. I didn't want to make any changes."

"So what changed your mind?"

"God," she said as she swiped a tear.

"Meaning?"

Another sigh slipped from her. "When I moved into that home for unwed mothers, I was a mess. Emotionally, spiritually, just a wreck."

Guilt nearly smothered him. No eighteen-year-old girl should have gone through what she did. He should have been there for her. Regret pierced him. If only he'd listened…

Even if she and Daniel had done something, Mason should have been able to put aside his own hurt and at least hear her out.

But he hadn't. His pride and hurt had flared to the point that he had been incapable of listening. And he couldn't change that. He could only work with the present.

She brushed away a stray tear. "I had a wonderful Christian counselor, Marie Beckham, who came to the home three times a week to talk to the girls. She used to be a resident there herself, so she knew what we were feeling—knew how to talk to us. Knew how to listen. She helped me get my self-esteem back. And while God and I didn't come to terms right away, Marie set me on the right path."

He reached out and stroked her cheek. "I'm so glad."

If only he could get the image of her and Daniel out of his mind. He needed to confront the man. Once and for all.

As soon as they found Bethany, he would.

Lacey took a deep breath. "Anyway, I started going to church—reluctantly, but I went, got a job, went to school at night, then had Bethany."

"When did you decide to move home?"

"When Bethany insisted on meeting her father." She ran a hand over her hair and looked away. "I wish I'd gotten up the nerve to talk to you before…."

"Yeah."

He took a deep breath and dropped his gaze to his hands. His phone rang and he grabbed it from the clip on his belt. It was Joseph.

"Hello."

"Hey, they're bringing our guy in now. He should be here in thirty minutes or so."

Mason looked at Lacey.

"All right, we'll be there shortly."

He hung up and Lacey looked at him with a question in her eyes.

"We need to get down to the interrogation room and see what this guy has to say."

Distaste crossed her face and he realized she was not looking forward to the confrontation. But she was determined to go through with it. Anything to find Bethany. Just another example of the kind of woman she was.

More doubts crowded him as they walked back down the hall. He had a feeling he'd made a terrible mistake sixteen years ago in refusing to move past his own hurt to listen to the girl he'd loved.

But that would have to wait. Pushing down his surging emotions, they entered the room and took a seat behind the two-way mirror.

Mason looked at Lacey who fidgeted with the strap of her purse. "Do you know how this works?"

She bit her lip. "Just from the TV version."

"It's not so different. They'll bring Howe and his lawyer in, present them with any evidence we have and start asking questions."

"She has to be okay, Mason." Lacey whispered the words and he had to strain to hear her. "She's been my whole life for fifteen years, the reason I got up in the mornings, the reason I didn't give up and crawl into a hole and die."

What could he say? He couldn't bring himself

to promise everything would work out. He'd seen too many times when it didn't. More times than it did.

Scooting his chair closer to hers, he grasped her hand and held it. She shot him a grateful look, glanced over his shoulder, then gasped. "There he is."

Mason turned to see John Howe and his lawyer enter the interrogation room. Howe walked with a pronounced limp—more so than when Mason had chased him and lost him—but he was walking under his own steam. Catelyn and Daniel brought up the rear.

Mason squeezed her fingers. "I'm going down there. I'll be back when we're done."

"They'll let you in?"

"Oh yeah, they'll let me in."

Lacey wasn't too sure, but didn't protest. She watched him leave, and a few minutes later he was allowed access to the room.

Catelyn didn't look surprised to see him. Daniel looked irritated, but didn't say anything.

After introductions and the lawyer's warning to his client not to answer until directed, they got started.

Daniel asked, "Why did you run when we showed up at your house?"

"Because I knew why you were there."

Lacey rocked back. He was admitting it? She admired the fact that Mason was able to keep a straight face. He jumped in.

"So where's Bethany?"

"Look," Howe sighed, "I'm cooperating with you because my lawyer convinced me it was in my best interest to cut a deal, but I tell you I don't know where the girl is. She got away from me."

Hope exploded through Lacey.

"Why did you try to take her in the first place?"

"I got a phone call from someone. That person asked if I wanted to make a lot of money." He squirmed. "I got debts to pay so I agreed."

"To kidnapping?" Catelyn asked.

"Well, not at first." He cleared his throat. "I didn't realize that's what I was agreeing to. I was just supposed to watch this girl and report back what she was doing, her daily routine, her relationship with her mother. I was the new guy at the karate school and I suppose this person knew Bethany went there. It was just supposed to be watching her, following her. You know—" he shrugged "—like surveillance stuff."

"Why?"

"I don't know. I didn't ask." He flushed. "I needed the money too much to worry about it."

"Who did you report to?"

"Same answer. I never met this person. Just

picked up my money from a different drop spot each time over a period of a month. Then, um, this person said they wanted me to grab the girl. I said no way. Then—" he blinked "—I got a letter with some pictures of my ex-wife and little boy. It said if I didn't follow through with everything they would disappear."

"So you went after Bethany."

He swallowed hard. "I didn't want to, but yeah." Tears appeared for a brief moment before he ducked his head. When he looked back up, they were gone. "I wasn't going to let anything happen to my son."

"Where'd you get the gun?" Daniel asked.

"It was left at one of the drop sites with half the money for grabbing the girl."

Lacey felt her stomach swirl and thought she might be sick. Mason looked ready to leap over the table and throttle the guy.

She admired his restraint.

Her hands ached and she realized she'd tightened her fingers into fists so tight her knuckles were white.

Making an effort to relax, she unfurled them and leaned toward the window.

A knock on the door pulled Catelyn from the interrogation as she moved to answer it. Someone Lacey couldn't see handed Catelyn a piece of paper. The detective looked at it and a smile of satisfaction crossed her face.

Turning back to the lawyer and Howe, she slid the paper across the table and said, "We have your print on the car Kayla Mahoney died in. What'd you do, John, run her off the road?"

"No!" he protested. "I was following behind them, yeah, but I didn't do anything that would make them wreck. All of a sudden the driver swerved then crashed into a tree."

That part matched with Georgia's story. So, it wasn't Austin Howard at the site of the wreck. Mason wasn't surprised.

"So you showed up, the girls thought you were there to help and you tried to get Bethany to go with you. When she wouldn't, you pulled the gun and ended up getting shot."

"Yeah." He rubbed shaking fingers across his lips. "That about sums it up."

"Not quite." Mason stood and slapped a hand on the table. "Did you leave that little gift in Bethany's room last night?"

Confusion flickered. "What are you talking about?"

Mason and Catelyn exchanged a glance. "You weren't anywhere near the Gibson household last night?"

"No and I have witnesses to prove it."

Daniel slid the man a pen. "Write them down."

Howe looked at his lawyer who'd been surprisingly quiet through the whole confession. The man nodded and Howe started writing.

When he was finished he set the pen down. "I don't know what happened to the girl. I was supposed to leave her drugged and tied to a tree out in the woods just at the edge of the high school. Then I was to pick up my money at another location about thirty minutes away at a specific time. I was warned not to be late or the money would be gone."

"While you were picking up the money, this person would be picking up Bethany," Mason stated in a low monotone. Howe nodded.

Lacey shuddered at the visual image.

Howe leaned back and sighed. "But it never happened. She got away from me." With a grudging respect, Howe admitted, "She's good at martial arts. I'm better, but she's good."

"So you've been looking for her, chasing her, right?"

This time a guilty flush appeared and he clamped his lips shut. His lawyer said, "Okay, that's enough questions. We're done here."

"Not quite." Mason leaned in and narrowed his eyes. "Bethany's out there all alone. She's scared and probably exhausted from trying to stay one step ahead of you. Why isn't she coming to us for help? Or at least finding the nearest cop?"

Howe averted his gaze.

Mason hit the table with a fist and everyone jumped.

"Hey…" the lawyer started to protest.

Mason ignored him and said softly, "You said you'd cooperate fully for a deal. If you have more information, you need to spill it."

Howe looked down at the table and swallowed, looked at his lawyer and sighed. "I used the girl's mother to get her to cooperate. I had a couple of pictures of Bethany's mom and showed them to her. I told her I was watching her mom. If she didn't do what I said, her mother would get hurt."

Rage exploded inside Lacey and it was all she could do to keep from bolting into the room to throttle the man. Even though Georgia had basically said the same thing, hearing it come from this man's mouth made her want to vomit.

A muscle jumped in Mason's jaw, but he held himself in control with admirable restraint. "I need the phone number of the person you were contacting."

Howe rattled it off and Mason glanced at Daniel who left the room.

To have it traced, Lacey supposed. Although she had a feeling it was going to be one of those prepaid phone deals that the police could never track down.

Depression settled on her shoulders. Another dead end.

Please, God, keep her safe. Lead us to her. Show us the way to find her. Let her know I'm looking and won't give up until I have her back.

"Oh—" Mason turned back "—one more question, if you don't mind. How did you get Bethany's cell phone number?"

Howe startled. "What?"

"Come on, don't play stupid. We found someone who saw her answer a phone and then run from you. Described, by the way, right down to your limp. So you might as well finish the story."

Howe's lawyer started to protest. Howe held up a hand. "It's all right." He flushed. "Yeah, I, um, got ahold of her again a couple of days ago. We struggled and my phone flew out of my pocket. She kind of snatched it as she was running away." He flushed then his lips flattened. "She caught me off guard with a kick to my bad leg or she never would have gotten away from me."

Lacey felt a surge of pride for her resourceful daughter. *Way to go, Bethany. Now use the thing to call me!*

"What's the number?" Mason demanded.

Howe gave it to him.

Mason stood and strode from the room pulling his cell phone out as he walked. Lacey leaped from the chair and raced from the room. She knew he was going to call Bethany. She'd call herself if she thought Bethany would answer, but she doubted she would if she was trying to protect her.

Rounding the corner, she almost ran into him. "Is she answering?"

Hanging up, he shook his head. "She's probably scared to. Probably thinks it's Howe."

"I don't guess you could leave her a message. She probably doesn't know the password to check them."

"She doesn't have a reason to check them even if she could." He shook his head. "I'll have the cell phone tracked. As long as she leaves the battery in, we'll be able to find her. If not, we'll have to find another way to locate her."

"But how?" she cried. "We don't have anything else that connects—"

She broke off as the captain came out of his office. He looked at Mason, then Catelyn and Daniel who'd come up the hall. Daniel spoke into his cell phone as the captain said, "We've got a tip that Bethany was seen at the homeless shelter."

Daniel's attention snapped to the captain. "The homeless shelter? We've got a black-and-white near there, don't we? Aren't they supposed to be covering that area?"

The captain nodded. "That's who called it in.

They didn't approach her because they didn't want to scare her. They're waiting for us."

"All right." Daniel looked at the captain, then Mason and Catelyn. "I've got another emergency to deal with. One of my other cases just caught a break. I really need to go take care of that." Into the phone, he said, "I've got to go. I'll call you later."

Catelyn nodded at Mason. "I'll drive."

The threesome headed for the exit, Lacey in the lead. Mason grabbed her arm. "I suppose it's futile to tell you to stay here."

Pulling out of his gentle grasp, she said, "You know it."

He gave a resigned sigh. "All right, but at least stay close by."

Relieved he didn't argue, she said, "Glad to."

And she was. The more she was around Mason, the more she wanted to be.

Climbing into the car, she closed her eyes. *Please, Jesus, let me find my daughter. Keep her safe. Keep us safe.*

When she opened her eyes, Mason was looking at her over his shoulder from the front passenger seat. "I'm praying, too."

She lifted a brow. "You are? I thought you and God weren't on speaking terms."

"I wouldn't say that. He was speaking to me, I just haven't been listening much—until now."

"Does Bethany have anything to do with your change of heart?"

He nodded. "Yeah. A lot."

The car turned and all conversations ceased as Catelyn spoke into her phone to let the other officers know they were there.

"Where is she?" Lacey craned her neck, desperate to catch a glimpse of her daughter. All she saw were two men walking toward the door.

A patrol car came up next to them. Catelyn rolled her window down and the officer said, "She's been pacing back and forth in front of the pay phone. Finally, she just went around the back."

Lacey jumped out of the car.

"Lacey!" Mason voiced his disgust with her. "Get back here."

She paused and looked at him. "Come on."

No sooner had the words left her lips than a crack sounded and something struck the ground beside her. Then the building spewed brick and cement and she felt the sting of it bite into her neck and upper arm.

FOURTEEN

In the time it took her to process the fact that someone was shooting at them, Mason snagged her hand and yanked her back into the car.

Screams echoed around her.

Hers intermingled with those of the people on the street.

In a blur Lacey watched Catelyn snatch her gun from her holster while Mason did the same. He yelled, "Where's it coming from?"

"Over there!" Catelyn pointed and called for backup, while bystanders frantically ducked behind whatever cover they could find.

Lacey felt her heart stutter as adrenaline pumped through her veins.

Bethany!

Where was she? Who was shooting at them? At her?

Mason no longer held her down and she risked a peek through the window when she heard sirens. Backup had arrived.

* * *

Mason bit back the frustration and anger as best he could. Would they never catch a break?

A dozen black-and-whites now covered the scene. If Bethany had been there, she was gone now. Catelyn had disappeared in the direction the bullets had come from. Mason ordered everyone to stay down. The scene hadn't been cleared yet.

Tears leaked from Lacey's eyes, and he felt her despair. His heart beat with a love it hadn't forgotten. The feeling shocked him and stirred him. With renewed hope, he realized that it might be possible to overcome the past. In one move, he pulled her to him and wiped her tears away. She sniffed and parted her lips to speak.

Before she could, he noticed the blood around the edge of the neck of her tank top.

"Are you all right?"

"No. I'm not," she whispered. "I won't be all right until Bethany is back."

"You're bleeding." Making his way to the trunk of the car, Mason pulled out a first-aid kit. Opening a bandage, he pressed it to her neck. She winced, and he said, "Sorry. Debris from the building got you."

"I felt it but didn't realize what it was." She shot him a grim smile. "Seems like you're patching me up quite a bit lately."

Through narrowed eyes, he regarded her. "Yeah, I don't like it."

"I can't say I'm real crazy about it myself."

Catelyn returned and, with a disgusted look, shook her head at Mason and Lacey. "Sorry. The shooter got away."

Lacey groaned.

Mason bit back a growl of frustration.

"Bethany?" he asked.

"She's gone, too," Catelyn replied.

Officers began reporting back that they'd found nothing. The scene was officially declared clear and a crime-scene unit arrived and began their job, while Catelyn began hers. Questioning those in the area.

Lacey looked at Mason. "What now?"

"We pray she calls. Come on, I'll take you home." He frowned. "Or to the hospital to get that checked."

"It's just a couple of scratches, Mason, I'll be fine."

Lacey's cell phone rang and hope flashed across her face. Snatching it from the pocket of her shorts, she looked at the screen and bit her lip. Her shoulders drooped.

It wasn't Bethany.

"Hello?"

Mason listened in on her conversation and refused to feel guilty about it.

"Yes, I know, Mr. Hill, I promise to get right on it. Bethany is still missing and—" She broke off then ended with, "Yes, sir. I will. Thank you."

Hanging up, she pulled in a deep breath.

"Your boss giving you a hard time?"

The smile she flashed him was forced. "Yes, but it doesn't matter. There are other jobs out there. I only have one Bethany."

Mason let himself admire her tenacity. She was determined to find her daughter no matter what it took. Too bad she hadn't put as much effort into telling him about Bethany as she was in finding the girl.

The brief thought hit him and he grimaced. *Don't go there, Stone.*

Shoving down those emotions, he motioned to Catelyn that he was taking the car. She nodded. He knew she'd grab a ride back to the station with one of the officers.

Mason helped Lacey into the passenger seat and then climbed behind the wheel.

The strained, drawn look on her face worried him. Dark circles had formed beneath her eyes and she looked ready to drop.

Going full steam ahead on very little sleep wasn't easy. He was used to it, but she wasn't.

"I want you to go home and rest."

She cut her eyes at him, but didn't protest. That in itself told him how exhausted she really was.

Ten minutes later, he pulled into her driveway. With a wave to the police cruiser assigned to watch her house, he walked her to the front door.

Placing his hands on her shoulders, he turned her to face him. "Hang in there, Lacey. I think we're getting close."

"How can you say that?" Doubt stared up at him.

"Just a gut feeling. The incidents are escalating. We may be making someone nervous."

"Nervous enough to hurt Bethany?" she whispered.

The quiet words cut a path of hurt through his heart and he pulled her close for a hug. "I sure hope not, but we can't stop looking. Bethany's counting on you to find her."

She gave a weary smile. "I know."

"Which means you can't collapse when we finally locate her. Go to bed."

The light in Lacey's eyes had dimmed to the point where it wouldn't take much for it to be snuffed completely out. She had to regroup. Recharge her body and let her racing mind rest.

He placed a kiss on her forehead and she blinked. "Good night, Mason."

"Night."

He watched her go and felt weariness creep

through him. He'd grab a couple of hours of rest, just enough to keep him going physically, then he'd be back at it.

Lacey's parents had gone out with some friends. That concerned her slightly as she was afraid the person who seemed to want to torment her would go after them. However, Lacey felt there would be safety in numbers and told her parents they needed the break.

Plus Mason had asked a fellow off-duty marshal to keep an eye on them. Carly Masterson. Lacey smiled. The woman was getting married soon and yet she'd immediately agreed to help Mason out. That said a lot about his friends and what they thought of him.

So her parents had gone.

Which left her home alone with a police officer bodyguard outside the front of the house.

Lacey grabbed some leftovers from her parents' supper the night before and absently warmed them up. Three bites of spaghetti and she was nauseous.

Fatigue, worry and anger at the person doing this pressed in on her. What had she *done* to this person to incite such hate?

All her life she'd played it safe, except for that one night with Mason when they'd ignored everything they'd been taught. One: don't put yourself in a place where it would be easy to give in to temptation. And two: flee temptation when you're hit with it.

Then she'd had a baby to take care of and no one except herself to lean on.

At least that's what she told herself.

Really, looking back, she saw where God placed people in her path all along her journey. The Christian counselor at the home, Mrs. Chisolm, who'd rented her one of her spare bedrooms, and then helped take care of Bethany after she was born.

Lacey had walked in on the woman studying her Bible or praying on many occasions. At first it had made her uncomfortable, then she found it sweet that the woman told Bethany Bible stories. As a result, she watched her daughter flourish under the older woman's love.

The love Lacey's mother should have been lavishing on Bethany.

But her parents hadn't mellowed the slightest until after Bethany's sixth birthday and by then Lacey was well and truly disconnected from them, except for the occasional card she felt compelled to write.

Until three years ago when she came to understand God's love. Not the kind of God her father preached about every Sunday, the one who was sitting in judgment ready to strike the minute she did something wrong, but a God who loved her just as she was—mistakes and all.

A God who forgave those mistakes and wanted to spend time with her. Actually wanted her to spend time with Him.

It had taken her a long time to accept that, but when she finally did, it was like opening up a whole new world for her.

She finally saw what she'd been missing.

Unconditional love.

The kind of love she tried to pour into Bethany.

The kind of love she hoped her parents would learn. And it seemed that prayer had been answered.

Being reconciled to her parents had had its ups and downs, but Lacey had decided to roll with the punches and accept the good times as they came. Sometimes her mother tried too hard and was overly solicitous. Most of the time it seemed as if her father just didn't know what to say to her. It caused Lacey pain when he wouldn't meet her eyes or would leave the room when she walked in.

Although, she had to admit, that seemed to be happening less. So, her plan seemed to be working.

Or it had been until Bethany disappeared.

With a sigh she took another bite of the spaghetti, working her way through the large portion until she finally managed to put a pretty good dent in it.

Snagging her laptop from the kitchen desk, she moved into the den and logged in to her work account. Thankfully her boss had decided she could work from home when there was nothing pressing in the office.

She needed to focus on the project. Needed to throw something else at her mind.

For the next hour and a half, she managed to keep her mind off Mason, although she periodically sent up prayers for Bethany. At least Bethany wasn't being held captive. She worked at a steady pace, designing the billboard she'd been assigned for a local radio station.

The stillness of the house finally registered.

Nerves jumping, she flashed to the memory of the wig stand in Bethany's room. The picture on the door. And the sting of her wounds reminded her that someone wanted to do her harm.

Shuddering, she set her laptop aside and rose to walk into the kitchen. She parted the blinds and looked in the direction of the police cruiser.

And relaxed a bit.

It was still there.

The ringing of the phone jarred her. Heart thudding she gave self-conscious laugh and snatched the handset from the base. "Hello?"

"Hello, Lacey. This is Janice."

Surprise shot through her. "Hi, Janice. How are you doing?"

"Good. But I just can't stand sitting around doing nothing while Bethany is missing. I wanted to see if I could help in some way."

Lacey allowed a weak smile to cross her lips. "That's very sweet, Janice. I appreciate it, but there's nothing anyone can do, short of going door to door asking if anyone has seen her."

There was a moment of silence. "I have an idea. I'm friends with a lot of store owners downtown. What if I take flyers and ask managers to post them in their windows?"

"Oh, Janice, that would be wonderful. Would you do that?"

"Sure. I'm not volunteering at the hospital tomorrow, Daniel will be working all hours and the Christmas store can wait because the air conditioner is *still* not fixed."

"Wonderful," Lacey said, her voice wobbling in spite of her best attempt to keep it steady. "We can share a cup of coffee, then get busy. Deal?"

"Deal."

Lacey felt tears prick her eyes. Grateful for her friend, she swallowed hard, momentarily unable to speak past the lump in her throat.

"All right then," Janice said, perky once again. "I'll see you tomorrow morning? My house? Nine o'clock?"

"Sure, Janice. See you then. And thank you."

Lacey hung up the phone. Placing her head in her hands, she prayed the flyers would make a difference.

But maybe Bethany would be home by then. *Please, God.*

It felt good to have a plan. To know she was going to be proactive in finding Bethany. But now, she had to focus on keeping her job.

Lacey sighed and went back to her laptop. Grabbing the yellow file from her briefcase, she searched for the sheet that would enable her to finalize the billboard ad.

It wasn't there.

She groaned. Where was it? Pulling everything from her briefcase, she went through each and every paper.

Nothing.

Closing her eyes, she thought.

Then remembered she'd left it on her desk the day of Bethany's disappearance.

In order to finish this and e-mail it to her boss tonight, she'd have to go to the office and retrieve the sheet from her desk.

Weariness grabbed her and held on tight. Did she want to do this now?

No.

But she needed to. She needed to keep this job. It was a good one and while she knew she had excellent skills and could find another job if she needed to, she didn't want to have to do the whole job-search thing again. Besides, she liked the work and the people in the office—including her boss.

And right now, there wasn't a thing she could do about finding Bethany. What she could do was ensure that she kept her job so she would be able support herself and Bethany when they finally brought her daughter back home.

Dragging herself to the kitchen counter, she grabbed her keys and headed for the door. After a stop to tell the officer where she was going and to reassure him she'd be fine, against his advice, she drove down the street and out of the subdivision. He'd offered to go with her and she'd almost let him, but what if her parents came home? They'd need him here. And she didn't want the house left sitting for any length of time without eyes on it.

If she let the officer go with her, there wouldn't be a deterrent to the person causing her family all this grief.

Hesitating, she thought about it. Was she being impulsive and thoughtless? Should she go to the office alone?

What if the person was watching her? What if he'd seen her leave and even now followed her?

Her eyes went to the rearview mirror and she breathed a sigh of relief at the darkness behind her.

A glance at the clock on the dash read 10:04 p.m. Should she call Mason?

For what?

She was just going to run in and grab that sheet then go home and finish the project. The office was well lit even at night. Plus there was the security guard. She'd get him to let her in and then see her back to her car. She'd be fine.

Lacey gave another cursory glance into the rearview mirror and sucked in a deep breath.

Headlights.

Her nerves tightened and she forced herself to relax. Just because someone was behind her didn't mean someone was *after* her. This was a well-traveled road.

Nevertheless, her fingers gripped the wheel and she cast another nervous eye toward the mirror.

Still there. And then the car went around her, zooming past to disappear around the curve ahead.

She breathed easier.

Another set of headlights pulled in behind her, but she didn't let it faze her. She was almost to the office.

However, while she told herself it was nothing, she couldn't help keep an eye on the rearview mirror.

Was it her imagination or was the car closer?

And coming closer with every passing second.

She flashed her brakes and made ready to make the last turn that would lead her to the office parking lot.

The car behind her slowed.

To follow her or just to avoid rear-ending her, she wasn't sure.

A drop of sweat dripped down from her hairline and with a start she realized exactly how scared she really was.

Where was her cell phone?

Her stomach dipped.

Had she left it at home?

No, she wouldn't do that. Bethany might call.

Her purse was on the backseat.

Could she reach back without running off the road?

Lacey made her turn and looked to see if the car followed.

It did.

Pulse now pounding in her throat, she gripped the wheel with her left hand and reached back with her right. On the third try, she managed to snag the strap and yank the purse to the passenger seat beside her.

Blindly, she searched the purse until her fingers curled around the vibrating phone.

Mason.

Shaking, her eyes still on the car behind her, she pressed the button to activate the call. "Mason," she blurted, "someone's behind me. I think he's following me. What do I do?"

"Pull into a parking spot. It's me behind you."

Relief nearly wilted her into a puddle in the seat. Then she got mad. "What are you doing following me? You nearly scared me to death!"

"Officer Bleddings decided he'd better call and tell me what you were up to. I decided to make sure you didn't get yourself killed."

Anger and thankfulness warred inside her. Disconnecting the call, she put the car in Park and opened the door.

Mason pulled into the space beside her and climbed out, his eyes flashing in the light of the streetlamp. "What do you think you're doing? Are you insane?"

Not giving her a chance to answer, he led her to the door and waited for her to unlock it. Once they were safely inside, he pulled her around to face him.

Crossing her arms in front of her she notched her chin up. "I'm not insane, although if we don't find Bethany soon, I may wind up that way. I was at home working on some stuff and I needed something from the office."

"Why didn't you call me?"

"Because I was hoping you were either trying to find Bethany—or asleep. I didn't want to disturb either one of those activities. And Pete, the security guard, is here—" she looked around and frowned "—somewhere."

Mason blew out a sigh and raked a hand through his hair. "Is Bethany anything like you?"

She blinked. Then smiled. "If you mean in the stubbornness department, then yes. Actually, more so."

He shook his head and she thought she heard him mutter, "I won't stand a chance."

When she gave a surprised giggle, his eyes darkened with something that looked suspiciously like tenderness. He moved closer and she gulped. Going still, she watched him, her heart thumping in anticipation of what she could see coming, what she welcomed. He didn't disappoint her as he pulled her close and slanted his lips across hers.

Time stood still as he offered her comfort, love—and a whole mix of feelings she wanted to explore. At a better time. In a different place. Mason must have sensed her slight emotional withdrawal because he lifted his head. "I suppose you still want to get what you came for."

Lacey sobered. "Yes. Working is helping keep

my mind occupied. I never stop thinking about her, but—" she shrugged "—it just helps."

His face softened in the light of the dim lobby lamp. "I understand."

She looked out of the window toward the parking lot. The darkness seemed ominous. The back of her neck tingled and she shivered. Mason's eyes shifted and the hand on her arm tightened. "Do you think someone's out there watching?" she whispered.

"I don't know, but I'll feel better once you get what you need and I deliver you safely home."

She nodded and looked around. "I wonder where Pete is. He's usually sitting right inside the door."

Mason's hand hovered over his weapon as he looked out the window.

Anxiety twisted inside her. "Do you see anything?"

"No."

"But you felt it, too, didn't you? You had that feeling of being watched."

"Yes. And that bothers me." He turned and ran a hand down her arm. With a start, she realized she had goose bumps the size of small mountains.

His touch didn't do a thing to diminish them. If anything, it added a few more. She shivered and stared up at him, the memory of that kiss still in the forefront of her mind. "Should you call the police?"

"For what? A suspicion?" Shaking his head, he patted his gun located in the shoulder holster on his side. "I'll keep watch. If I think we need some help, I'll call for it. Get what you need and let's get out of here."

Lacey nodded and headed down the hall to her office, wondering once again where Pete was.

"Pete? Are you here?"

No answer.

Pulling out her key card again, she started to slide it through the slot and found her door cracked.

Puzzled, she pushed it open and flicked the light on. Looking around, she didn't see anything out of place. Moving to her desk, she flipped the small lamp on and started opening her mail. Might as well see what she'd missed over the last couple of days.

"Hey, Ms. Gibson, what are you doing here?"

Lacey looked up. "Pete. I wondered where you were. Is everything all right?"

The fifty-something gray-headed man with the round belly scratched his chin. "Sure, I was just in the restroom when I heard the door chime."

She smiled at him. "I just came to get something to finish up a project. I have a friend with me."

"Yeah, I met him. Nice fellow." He waved a

hand in the direction of the front of the building
"I'll just be in my office if you need anything."

Lacey nodded and went back to her mail.

The last piece was an interoffice envelope. She
opened it, reached in and pulled out the content.
A younger version of herself gazed back at her
from the picture. She gasped, letting the photo
fall to the desk.

"What is it?"

She whirled to find Mason standing at the door
frowning.

"Someone sent me more hate mail."

"What do you mean?" He moved closer.

She backed away from the desk. "Another
picture."

Only this one was of her and Bethany seated
at an outdoor café, oblivious to the fact that they
were being watched.

Lacey clenched a fist and stuffed it against her
mouth. Anger clamored inside her. Pointing at the
picture, she asked, "Why? I don't understand. I
the person doing this would just send me a letter
telling me what I've done…"

Mason placed his hands on her shoulders.
"Lacey, unfortunately, I don't think the person
doing this is reasonable—or even sane."

Lacey leaned into his chest and wrapped her
arms around him. She needed comfort right now
and he was offering it. "What do we do now?"

He pulled in a breath as he reached for his phone. "Let me call Catelyn and Daniel and we'll get them here to process your office. However, if that came through the interoffice mail, my guess is that our perp never set foot in this office. We'll need to question Pete, too, but if it came during the day, he wouldn't know anything about it."

After he made the call, Lacey grabbed the sheet she needed from the side of her desk and shook her head. "I don't know. I'm so tired of having this person one step ahead of me every time I turn around. How did he know I'd be in my office today? This was totally spur of the moment."

"When was that sent?"

She looked at the date stamp and pulled in a deep breath. "The day after Bethany disappeared."

"So, it's been here all this time."

Lacey groaned then looked at the picture once more. "I can't believe all this," she whispered.

"Come on," Mason urged. "I'll take you home. Catelyn and Daniel will take care of your office, talk to Pete and fill you in on anything they find." A thought seemed to hit him. "Are there any security cameras around here?"

Lacey thought. "Just on the front entrance and the back door. I don't think they have any in the halls or anywhere else."

"All right, it was just a thought." A car door

slammed and Mason headed for the front doo
"That's got to be Daniel and Catelyn."

Mason let them in and after explaining th
picture, motioned for Lacey to join him in th
hall. "Do you have what you need to finish you
project?"

"Yes." She gripped the sheet, wondering if she'
even be able to work anymore tonight.

After extracting the promise from Catelyn t
call if they learned anything, she was back in he
car with Mason following behind her. Still, sh
couldn't help but examine every road she passe
every car that pulled up beside her at a red ligh

When she turned into the drive, he pulled i
behind her, got out and walked her to the doo
They stepped inside and he shut it behind him.

Taking her hand in his, he stopped her fror
going farther into the foyer. She looked up a
him. He said, "It's going to be all right, Lacey,
promise."

"You can't make that promise, Mason, bu
thanks."

He dipped his head in acknowledgment to he
words then leaned down and placed a light kis
on her upturned lips.

Shocked, she went still and stared up at hin
"Mason?"

"I've never gotten over you, Lace," he said
conflicting emotions clearly displayed in his blu

yes. His husky voice set her heart to shimmering and her pulse to racing. Clearing his throat, he stepped back. "After we find Bethany, can we have that long-overdue talk?"

Lacey's heart flashed a cautious warning. He still didn't believe her about Daniel. Or maybe he did, he just wasn't willing to admit it yet. Surely he'd noticed how she didn't want to be around Daniel, how she found excuses not to double-date with him and whoever he was dating. She looked at Mason and sighed. Then again, maybe he hadn't. He'd always had a blind spot where his friend was concerned. "We can talk," she promised.

Relief flickered across his face and Lacey practically shoved him out the door. Her pulse pounded. Her lips tingled. She'd wanted to throw herself into his arms and forget the past. But she couldn't do that. She had to protect herself against the possibility that Mason wouldn't truly be able to believe her when she said she was innocent of leading Daniel on.

Blowing out a sigh, she said goodnight to her parents and hurried to her room. She placed her laptop and the sheet she'd just retrieved from her office on the small desk under the window. Her eyes fell on the picture next to the laptop. The one of her and Bethany when her daughter was around twelve years old.

She picked up the picture and stroked the small cheek forever encased behind the glass. "Oh, baby, where are you?"

Her heart ached for Bethany so much she thought it might crack wide open.

Through sheer force of effort, she refused to think of all the horrid things that could be happening to her daughter. Instead, she focused on the good thoughts. Memories of the times when she and Bethany spent time laughing together. Just the two of them.

Another picture smiled back at her from the desk. This one had Bethany decked out in her karate uniform, arms up, fists balled, ready to defend herself.

"Ah, Bethany, I'm sorry you feel like you have to put yourself in danger to protect me."

She looked at the sheet in her hand then turned to look at the Bible on the nightstand.

Carrying the picture with her, she settled on the bed and picked up the Bible.

Work could wait. Bethany needed her prayers and that's what she was going to get.

"Daddy, help me! Where are you?" Mason heard the words, but he couldn't find the source. Gun drawn, he raced into the building.

"Bethany, I'm coming, darling, I'm coming!"

"Daddy! Why won't you help me?" The tone turned accusing, the hurt piercing his heart.

"I'm coming," he assured her. "Just tell me where you are!"

Then she was before him, her eyes glaring, finger pointing. "You weren't there. You were never there. You should have listened to my mom. Why didn't you listen? I'll never forgive you."

Her eyes welled with tears and grief twisted inside him. "I'll listen, Bethany, I promise. I'll listen."

A crackle of laughter louder than thunder shattered the air and Mason whirled to see Daniel standing behind Bethany, an arm around her shoulders. "You're a loser, Stone. Lacey never wanted you. Only me. And now her daughter feels the same."

Wait, how did she get behind him?

He spun back to find Lacey standing there, tears running down her cheeks. "Why didn't you listen, Mason? You should have listened. Look at what you missed. You missed it all because you wouldn't listen." Her voice started to fade. "You should have listened."

With a jerk, he woke up, breaths coming in shallow pants. Sweat dripped from his hair. Kicking aside the tangled sheets, he stumbled from his bed wondering what the dream meant. He shuddered and tried to push the remnants from his mind.

This was the second time he'd had the dream and he started to worry it might become a regular occurrence unless he and Lacey worked things out. He scraped a hand across his jaw. He needed a shave.

He'd tossed and turned, the short four hours he'd actually dozed passing in a haze of dreams. Not only had he dreamed of Bethany and Lacey, he'd relived his wild chase through the restaurant parking lot. He alternated between saving Bethany from her kidnappers and not being able to reach her in time.

Still drenched from his tortuous night, he hit the shower for the longest one he'd had in a while.

While dressing, he decided to drive back by the homeless shelter and prayed he'd spot Bethany. It seemed to be where she turned when in need of a place to sleep.

The staff of the shelter had been alerted to call the police if she showed up, but so far there'd been no reports.

And those pictures from the wreck. He couldn't get them out of his mind. Not only did his heart break for Kayla's parents, but for the other two girls involved.

In a spontaneous move, he grabbed the phone and dialed Daniel's number.

"Hello?"

"Daniel, it's Mason. I need to see those accident pictures one more time."

The man scoffed. "Come on, Stone, what do you think you're going to find that the rest of us haven't?"

Mason felt his jaw harden. "I don't know, Daniel, but I just thought I'd like to go over them again. Do you think you could put aside your skepticism and work with me on this?"

For a moment Daniel was silent. Then a sigh filtered through. "Yeah, you're right." Another pause. "Bethany's your daughter, isn't she? That's why you're on this case."

This time it was Mason's turn to hesitate, but he wasn't going to lie. "Yes, she is."

"I thought so. Looking at her picture then looking at you…it's pretty obvious."

"So—" Mason changed the subject "—you want to meet me at the office so I can look at the pictures one more time?"

"They're not there. I brought the files home with me. Why don't you come over here and we'll take a look."

Mason grabbed his car keys. "I'll be right there."

FIFTEEN

Lacey pulled up to the Ackerman's house in one of the nicer areas of town. But she couldn't shake the feeling she was being watched.

She shivered in the summer heat and looked around before opening the car door. Had someone followed her to the house?

If so, that meant somebody had been watching. Waiting for her to leave her house.

A little nauseous at the thought, she hurried up the front walk and rapped on the door.

Janice answered right away, looking chic and attractive in her matching pants and top and various accessories. Lacey felt like a frump in her jeans and T-shirt. Some things never changed.

"Good morning, Lacey." The woman took Lacey's hand and pulled her inside. "Thank you for coming over. Have you heard anything from Bethany?" Concern lined Janice's face and Lacey appreciated that.

Forcing a tight smile, she shook her head. "Nothing yet."

Daniel appeared in the doorway. "But we're working on it. Mason's on his way over to look at the accident pictures again." He looked at Janice. "We'll be downstairs in my office."

Janice rolled her eyes then looked at Bethany. "All he does is work." Then she bit her lip. "But I guess for you and Bethany that's a good thing."

Lacey nodded. "Definitely." Then her heart picked up a little speed. Mason was on his way over. She rubbed her hands together and ordered the butterflies in her stomach to settle down.

"Well, come on in the kitchen," Janice said, "and we'll have a little chat along with some coffee."

Not really in the mood for either, Lacey nevertheless followed her high school friend into the kitchen and sat at the oval table. The kitchen boasted granite countertops, state-of-the-art appliances and hardwood floors. "Your home is beautiful."

A wry smile twisted Janice's lips. "Well, don't think all this came from Daniel's salary or what little profit I make at the store." She sighed. "No, my father asked me what I wanted for Christmas last year and I told him—a new kitchen." She waved a hand and shook her head. "And so that's what I got."

Lacey blinked. "You know, Janice, growing up I don't remember your dad being quite so generous with his money. What changed?"

Janice shot her a look beneath perfectly mascaraed lashes. "A lot has happened since high school. I had a bad time of it for a while and my father came to the rescue."

Janice poured them both a cup of coffee and sat opposite Lacey. Lacey added cream and sugar and stirred the steaming liquid.

Wrapping her hands around the mug, Janice said, "So, enough about me. I hear they caught the man who tried to kidnap Bethany."

After taking another sip, Lacey nodded. "Yes, but he said he was just following orders, that the person who hired him threatened his family if he didn't kidnap Bethany. He also said he doesn't have a clue who the person was, so he's been no help at all."

The woman raised a brow. "Well, why not? He got her this last time he went after her, didn't he?"

Lacey shook her head. "Apparently not. He said Lacey got away from him."

"Then why hasn't she called you?" Disbelief wrinkled her forehead into a frown.

"Because I think she's too afraid."

"Of what?"

Lacey sighed. She didn't really want to talk

about it, but maybe rehashing it would help sort some things out in her mind.

A knock on the door interrupted her and there went the butterflies again. Mason was here.

Her eyes focused on the doorway from the kitchen that led to the foyer. Daniel's heavy tread sounded and soon she heard the men greeting each other.

Soon the footsteps headed toward the kitchen and Mason and Daniel stood there. For a brief moment an awkward silence descended until Mason shot a smile and said, "Good morning, ladies."

Lacey's pulse pounded. He was so handsome—even though he looked like he hadn't had a good night's sleep since she'd knocked on his door. He probably hadn't. "Good morning, Mason." She frowned. "What do you think you're going to find in those pictures that we haven't already discovered?"

"Thank you," Daniel said. "I asked him the same thing."

Mason's eyes glittered for a moment then he shrugged. "I don't know, but it never hurts to be too careful."

"Well, I'll agree with that one," Janice murmured.

"I'll tell you if I find anything, Lacey."

He must have seen her agitation. Her desire to

ask to come with them. She shifted and nodded She wouldn't be rude to Janice.

Mason and Daniel left, and Lacey simply stared after them, thinking. Would Mason confron Daniel about the past while he had him down-stairs? Would Daniel come clean about it and admit everything?

Her heart trembled at the thought of Danie vehemently denying that he was the one that had come on to her back in high school. That he'd se her and Mason up. And at this point, why would Mason all of a sudden decide to believe her and not his friend?

Please, God, she whispered silently.

"Lacey?"

She blinked. "Oh, sorry. Right." She took a deep breath. "The man threatened to kill me if Bethany tried to contact me. I think she's staying hidden in order to protect me. And yet it appears that I've done something to make someone really mad so they're coming after me, anyway."

"Oh, you poor thing. I'm so sorry."

"So," Lacey said with a forced brightness, "what's been going on with you since we last stayed up all night talking about boys and eating pizza?"

Janice gave a small laugh. "Well, let's see. Daniel and I got married about two years after you left town." She took a sip of coffee. After she set the cup back on the table she said, "It took me that long to convince him you weren't coming back. He was crazy about you in high school, but you only had eyes for Mason."

Lacey felt her cheeks flush. Daniel had caused her a lot of grief back then and even if she had come back home before now, she would have avoided him like the plague.

But she didn't tell Janice that. She wasn't sure Janice knew the whole story or quite possibly the *true* story of what went on between her and Daniel.

And she wasn't going to be the one to tell her. "You've been married a long time. Did you decide not to have children? I remember we used to look at baby stuff in the stores. You had names all picked out. Megan for a girl and Cody for a boy."

Grief flashed in Janice's eyes, and Lacey immediately wished she could take the question back.

Janice blinked against the tears that had sprung to her eyes. "Oh, I wanted children, make no mistake about that. And we almost made it, but…" She sighed and traced a finger around the edge of her cup. "I was pregnant about six years ago. Around Christmastime, we had a big ice storm. I was leaving the house when I fell down the front porch steps. I was seven months along."

"Oh, no! I'm so sorry."

The woman nodded. "I lost the baby, a little girl and had to have an emergency hysterectomy." She shuddered and closed her eyes. "My little Megan," she whispered. She opened her eyes and shook her head. "It was horrible. I'm still not over it." Drawing in a deep breath, Janice cocked her head and looked unseeing out the window. "I think if I hadn't had to have the hysterectomy, I might have had hope that I could conceive again, but—" she shrugged "—that didn't happen. I had no hope." This time a tear trickled down her cheek, and Lacey reached a hand across to grasp Janice's fingers.

"What about adoption?" she asked. "Obviously money's not a problem for you…."

"It may sound selfish, but I didn't want someone else's baby. I wanted mine." She tapped a finger to her chest and sniffed. Lacey couldn't stand it anymore and rounded the table to wrap her arms around Janice's shoulders.

The woman let her hug her for a minute then patted her hand and pulled away. "Enough of this stuff. It's in the past. Let's brainstorm what we can do to find Bethany. I want to meet her."

Lacey pulled in a deep breath and took a sip of her coffee. It needed more sugar. She reached for the bowl. "I would love for you to meet her. Hopefully one day soon, you can."

The phone on the wall rang. Janice glanced

at it and sighed. "I'll have to get that since Daniel's downstairs. He has a separate line for his office."

"That's fine."

Janice answered the phone and Lacey heard her say, "All right, I'll be right there."

She hung up and turned to Lacey with a distressed sigh. "I'm terribly sorry. You're going to think I'm so rude, but I have to go to the store. That was the air-conditioning man and he says I have to sign some papers."

Lacey stood, relieved. "That's fine. I understand. We'll just plan to do this again after Bethany's home and you can meet her, all right?"

"Sure." Lacey stood and Janice waved her back into the chair. "No, no. Finish your coffee and then you can just see yourself out. No hurry, okay? I'll take the flyers with me and pass them out while I'm there."

"Oh, okay. Thanks."

Janice turned into a whirlwind and was soon out the door.

Lacey took another swallow of her coffee, picked up the newspaper that had been discarded onto the table and realized what she was doing.

Subconsciously, she realized that if she hung around long enough, Mason would come upstairs. She flushed at her teenage actions then frowned.

Maybe she'd just make her way downstairs and see what the men were working on. No doubt it had something to do with Bethany.

She left the kitchen and walked into the family room. Just as she reached the steps located on the far end of the room, she heard footsteps coming up.

Mason appeared with his cell phone stuck to his ear and stopped short when he saw her. "Bethany? Just tell me where you are so I can come find you."

"Bethany!" Lacey cried as she darted to his side, hope and joy filling her.

Mason nodded, his eyes intense. He put her on speaker phone so the others could hear. Lacey waited for the sound of her daughter's voice.

"I—I can't." A muffled sob. "He'll kill her."

"She's right here with me, Bethany. I'm not going to let anything happen to her, I promise. Now tell us where you are."

"Let me speak to her." Lacey reached for the phone.

Mason shook his head and gave her the "wait a minute" signal, one finger raised.

Daniel also had his cell phone out and nodded to Mason.

What did that mean?

Impatience raged through her. She wanted, no, *needed* to speak to her daughter. "Please!"

Mason shook his head again. "Bethany, I'm your father, okay?"

A gasp came through the line and Lacey felt her stomach swirl. That hadn't been the way she wanted to break the news, but maybe it was the right way. The only way. The way to get Bethany to tell them where she was.

Then Bethany said, "How? What's your name? Why do you have Georgia's phone?"

"Your mother came to me when you disappeared. My name's Mason Stone and I'm a U.S. Marshall, okay? One part of my job is to find people. I've been looking for you since you disappeared."

For a moment, all that was heard was Bethany's labored breathing.

Mason tried again. "I've been wanting to meet you ever since your mom told me about you. Now, who's after you, Bethany?"

"I don't know," she cried. "But I can't let them hurt my mom. Okay?"

"No one's going to hurt her. She's standing right here."

He handed her the phone and shot another look at Daniel who waved his hand as if to say keep going.

Lacey pulled the phone to her and said, "Bethany? Honey, I love you so much. Where are you? Please tell us where you are?"

"Mom! I'm sorry," the girl blurted. Lacey heard the tears in her voice. "I'm so sorry. I can't let him hurt you."

"It's okay, baby. Is it the guy with the limp? He's been arrested. Now tell me where you are."

Bethany gave another little gasp. "Arrested?" Hope shimmered in her voice. "Oh, good. That's so good." Lacey's heart nearly broke as her daughter gave a hiccupping sob. "I'm at a pay phone across the street from the homeless shelter. There's a place around the corner that serves free meals."

Mason grabbed Lacey's arm and ushered her toward the door. She followed at a quick pace, and soon they were in his car racing toward the shelter. Daniel led the way.

Bethany gave a gasp. "On, no! There's that car again. I thought you said he'd been arrested!"

"What car?" Mason snatched the phone from Lacey.

"The one that always seems to find me when I'm around here!"

"Describe it for me, quick."

"Um. I don't know. It's a white Buick. It's coming closer!"

"Can you see what the driver looks like?"

"No. The windows are dark. I can't…"

Mason's jaw looked like granite as Lacey's stomach twisted inside itself. Prayers floated from her lips as Mason instructed, "Bethany, I want you to run into a crowded place like the nearest restaurant or the shelter. Wait until you don't see the car anymore then call me back on Georgia's phone, all right?"

"All ri—Hey! Ouch!"

"Bethany!"

Faintly they heard, "Why'd you do that?"

"Bethany, what happened?"

No answer.

"Bethany!" he hollered again.

Nothing but nerve-shattering silence answered him.

SIXTEEN

Seven minutes later, Mason spun the wheel to the right and followed Daniel's car around the curve, breathing a sigh of relief as the homeless shelter came into sight.

Immediately, he saw the pay phone Bethany had called from. The receiver hung off the hook, gently swaying back and forth. His relief faded as his stomach dipped and his heart picked up speed. Lacey's distressed breaths echoed through the car as she craned to get a look at the pay phone. "Where is she? Where is she?"

Mason felt sick. They were too late.

It wouldn't stop them from looking, but he knew they were too late. Someone had grabbed her. Police cars had already started to arrive on the scene. Three pulled up in front of the homeless shelter.

Lacey pointed. "The phone."

He didn't tell her he'd already seen it. "Keep

our eyes open. She may be hiding nearby." He wanted to believe it…but didn't.

Lacey jumped out of the car the minute he pulled to a stop next to the curb. He didn't bother to stop her. Whatever danger had been here had already claimed its victim today.

Bethany.

Daniel began issuing orders. "Question all the residents of the shelter. I'll start with her, she's a regular and pretty friendly with the cops." He flagged a ragged-looking woman down and asked, "Helen, did you see anything over there by the pay phone?"

"Like what?" She tilted her head and gave Mason and Lacey the once-over.

"Like someone attacking a teenage girl and forcing her to go with them."

Helen shrugged. "Nope. Sorry. I just got here a minute ago."

"That's about when this happened," Lacey muttered.

Daniel sighed and walked away. He spoke into his microphone and someone squawked an answer. Mason planted his hands on his hips and watched the action. Officers questioned suspects. The crime-scene unit finally arrived, and he grabbed Lacey's hand to pull her next to him.

He turned to speak to one of the officers. When he turned back around, she was gone.

* * *

Lacey watched Daniel disappear around the phone booth and decided to follow him. She knew she might get yelled at, but had to know if he'd found anything.

Sidling up next to him and the other officer, she listened unashamedly.

"...a syringe."

"Where?" Daniel asked.

"On the ground, underneath the receiver. What did you get?"

"Nothing of any importance, but we'll check it out anyway." With a gloved hand, Daniel shoved a multicolored piece of material into a brown paper bag and folded the top over.

Lacey turned when Mason walked up beside her, his face a thundercloud. She looked at Daniel. "Is that syringe a clue?"

"I don't know. I'll have the lab check it out." He stuffed it into a paper bag and handed it to the tech standing nearby.

Then he turned to Mason. "I called Catelyn and asked her to pull up every white Buick registered within a thirty-mile radius."

"Good." Mason pulled Lacey to the side. "Lacey, I understand you're anxious to find Bethany, but if you get in the way of the investigation, you could hinder it and that's not going to help Bethany."

Guilt hit her. He was right. She was acting

impulsively, her desperation to find Bethany short-circuiting her usual calm, rational thought. Biting her lip she looked at the ground. "I'm sorry."

A finger under her chin tilted her face up to look into his compassionate gaze. "I know. We just need to be careful, all right?"

She nodded and he sighed, pulled her next to his chest and placed a kiss on her head. "We're going to find her."

If the determination in his voice was anything to go by, they would have Bethany back in no time. Unfortunately, she had a hard time believing this.

"But now someone has her. For real this time. She's not just out there on the run able to come home any time she decides to." Tears clogged her throat yet again and she swallowed hard.

"Hey, Mason!" Daniel called.

Mason turned and Lacey peered around him to see an officer escorting one of the residents of the shelter. A clean-cut young man in his early twenties. Lacey decided he looked rather out of place for a shelter resident, but she supposed they didn't all have to look like ragged misfits.

The officer, whose nametag read P. Hines, and the man stopped in front of them. The young man nodded and shoved his hands in his front pockets. Officer Hines said, "Troy here saw something. I'm going to let him describe it to you."

Troy shuffled his feet then shrugged. "I was heading out to look for a job and saw a girl near the pay phone over there. It looked like someone ran into her. She turned around to yell at the guy, then she dropped the phone and looked kind of sick. That's when a woman approached her. The girl looped her arm around the woman's neck and they walked off together."

Lacey's questions burned holes in her mind, but she kept her mouth shut and let the professionals handle it. Mason asked, "Did you recognize the guy?"

"No, he had his back to me and when the girl started yelling at him, he took off down the street."

Mason nodded. "All right, what about the woman and the girl. Did you see where they went?"

Troy shook his head. "Naw, I wasn't paying that much attention once I saw the girl had some help. I started walking down the sidewalk. Then I saw all the police cars headed this way and thought I'd turn around and come back to find out what was going on."

Lacey pulled in a deep breath, relief filling her. "She had help?"

"Looked like it to me." He shrugged.

"Anything else you can remember?"

"No, but, um—" he scratched his head "—seems

like I remember seeing Billy Rose around. You might ask him if he saw anything."

"Thanks," Mason nodded. "We'll do that."

Daniel looked confused, troubled. Lacey looked at him. "What is it?"

He jerked. "Nothing. Just thinking." He looked at Troy. "You said she looked sick." Troy nodded. Daniel looked at Mason. "We found a syringe."

"You think she was drugged."

"It's possible. The syringe certainly indicates that."

"And this woman just came out of nowhere to help her," Mason said flatly.

Daniel shook his head. "I don't buy it." He held two bags, one that contained the piece of material he'd found and the other the syringe. "I'll get these to the lab and beg for a rush on the contents of the syringe."

"But if the person in the white car got out, Bethany would have run. Instead, she stayed on the phone, watching the car. Then she said 'ouch.'" Lacey frowned, trying to work through a possible scenario of what had happened. She had to. Dwelling on the fact that she'd once again lost Bethany was killing her.

Mason rubbed his lips and nodded. "I agree. So the person who jabbed her with the syringe didn't expect help to come along. Whoever the woman was that helped Bethany probably saved her life. Now we just have to find out who the woman is."

"Who hates me so much?" Lacey whispered. "And—" she lifted her hands, palms up "—why?"

Daniel pursed his lips and looked at her. "You've really made an enemy in this town. Anyone in particular come to mind?"

"Just you," she blurted, then spun on her heel and stomped to the car.

Surprise slugged Mason like a baseball bat to the gut. As soon as the words left her mouth, he could tell she regretted them.

But they made him think.

Shooting Daniel a look, he said, "I'll be in touch. Let me know what you find out about the syringe and the white Buick, will you?"

Daniel's jaw looked tight enough to shatter, but he managed to mutter, "Sure."

Mason caught up with Lacey at the car. She had her elbows resting on the hood with her face buried in her hands. Praying? Probably. "Are you all right?"

"No. I shouldn't have said that to Daniel. I owe him an apology," she mumbled into her palms. "I'm very ashamed of myself right now."

He sighed. "Do you really think Daniel would do the things that have happened to you?"

She looked up, eyes weary. He thought if he could see her soul, even it would look tired. She gave a tiny shrug. "I don't know. He's the only one I can think of that might be threatened by my return to town."

"Why would you coming back here be a threat to him?"

Biting her lip, she looked away for a brief moment, then back. Straightening her shoulders, she said, "Because only two people know the truth about that day you found us together. One person wants the world to know that story. The other doesn't."

Skepticism found its way into his mind and by the look on her face, he didn't hide it very well.

She waved a hand and gave a humorless laugh. "Why do I keep trying?"

"Lacey, I'm sorry. Daniel has been nothing but a friend to me. He was there in elementary school with me the day my mom left. He was the only one who understood because his mom left, too. We had a bond that—" He shrugged. "I can't really explain it."

She'd known Daniel's mother had left shortly before Mason's had, but hadn't realized that had been the reason they'd become fast friends. No wonder Mason had such loyalty to the man. Loyalty to a man who'd once been a teenager who had betrayed his friend. Too bad Daniel didn't feel the same way about Mason that Mason did about him.

But how did she convince Mason of this? Part of her wondered why she even had to convince him. Why did it matter if he believed her or not?

The only answer she could come up with was because she cared. Because she'd never stopped loving him and wanted another chance with him.

Her heart squeezed. *Oh, Lord, don't let me get hurt again. And open his eyes to the truth. I think only You can do that now.*

"Then I'm not going to try to convince you."

"Lacey…"

"What's next?"

He sighed. To her frustration—and relief—he let it drop. She'd just have to continue to earn his trust. Show him she would never be like his mother. And pray. Pray that God revealed the truth to him and opened his eyes.

He reached over and opened the passenger door. "All right, let's go. I'll take you home. There's nothing more we can do here."

Lacey looked back the pay phone. Her last connection with Bethany. She was loathe to leave it, but deep down she knew Bethany wasn't coming back here.

She climbed in and Mason shut the door with a snap.

When he crawled in the driver's side, Lacey firmed her jaw and took a deep breath. "Okay, I know I said I wasn't going to try to convince you that I'm telling the truth and Daniel is lying through his teeth. I really wasn't planning on getting into this, but I want you to hear the whole story. I've protested my innocence until I'm blue in the face. If you choose not to believe me, so be it. But here's the truth whether you want to hear it or not."

Surprise lifted his brow and he did a double take. She blundered on. "That day, I was going to wait for you after school like I always did. On that bench under the tree behind the gym. That day you told me you'd be running a little late and had to meet with your calculus teacher. Remember?"

He nodded. "Yeah. I do. I'd missed a test because of the flu and had to schedule a time to make it up."

"So I took my time getting there. When I arrived, Daniel was already there."

A frown flitted across his forehead, but at least he was listening.

"He knew I was waiting for you because he said 'Looks like we have a little time to talk before Mason gets here.'"

"Talk about what?"

"I don't even remember now. He patted the seat beside him, I do remember that. So we talked a bit, then all of a sudden he said he had something in his eye and asked me if I would look at it."

Mason scoffed, but without heat. "That's the oldest trick in the book. You fell for that?"

She felt the flush creep up. "I wasn't thinking anything except he looked like he had something in his eye. Up to that point, he didn't act like he was hitting on me or anything. I leaned over. He kept leaning farther back. Then all of a sudden, I felt him tug on me and I lost my balance. I landed practically on top of him and he started kissing me. When I tried to pull away, he held me down. And then you were there."

Silence filled the car. Then she whispered. "You can believe me or not, but that's the truth."

"But why?"

His cry nearly ripped her heart in two.

"Because he was jealous of you. He wanted to drive us apart. And he knew the one thing that would do it." She gulped. She had to tell him all of it. "He saw you coming and said, 'If I can't have you, Mason sure isn't going to.'" A tear dripped off her chin.

Mason felt the anguish fill him.

She wasn't lying to him.

After spending the last couple of days together, he'd seen a lot of what she was experiencing go

cross her face to land in her eyes. Deceit wasn't
ne of the things revealed there.

It took him a moment to process that he'd
elieved a lie all these years. He stared at her.
Blinked. "I believe you."

He'd shocked her into silent stillness.

Reaching across the car, he took her hand. "I
elieve you."

Still, she simply stared at him. Her mouth
vorked and nothing came out. Finally, she
queaked, "You do? Why?"

"Why?" He gave a choked laugh. "Because I'm
ooking at you and thinking I know you so well
nd I remember who you were. I see who you've
ecome and you're not lying—I believe you."

A whimper escaped her. Then tears welled and
egan to roll down her cheeks. "Really?"

"Really. And I'm sorry," he whispered back,
eeling his own throat go tight. "I'm so very
orry."

She nodded and swiped her cheeks. Lean-
ng over, he placed a hand behind her head and
ulled her in to close his lips over hers. A soft
igh escaped her and she didn't resist. Gratitude
illed him. He meant the kiss to reassure her, to
e a promise, to renew hope that they could still
ave a life together. *Please, God.*

His heart smiled at the short prayer.

When he pulled back, he zeroed in on her

flushed cheeks and soft eyes. "We've got a lot t
talk about. A lot to plan. But first…"

"…we find our daughter," she finished.

"Yeah." He nodded. His heart beat with unr
strained love for this amazing woman. Regr
and anger pierced him as he thought about th
lost years, but he pushed them aside with dete
mined force. Nothing was going to dampen wha
was building at lightning speed between him an
Lacey.

After one last lingering kiss, he gave her so
cheek a gentle stroke. When he turned back t
crank the car, emotion blindsided him. Pullin
in a deep, steadying breath, he said, "Right. W
find our daughter." Then his jaw hardened. "An
I have a heart-to-heart with Daniel Ackerman."

SEVENTEEN

Mason dropped her off at home and left. She chewed the inside of her lip as she watched him drive away. And frowned.

She waved to the unmarked car sitting on the curb. Mason had called in a friend of his. Another marshal giving up her day off to keep an eye on things at Lacey's house.

Her heart clenched with gratitude. She was very blessed in spite of her daughter's disappearance. She just had to keep reminding herself of this fact.

Entering the house, she found her parents in the den watching the news. Probably hoping to hear Bethany had been found.

"Hi," she said softly.

Her father looked up, his lined face seemed to have a acquired a few more wrinkles just in the short amount of time Bethany had been missing. "Anything?"

"We thought we had caught her, but—" She bit

her lip and shook her head. "I'm not sure what to think. It seems she was attacked, then rescued by a woman. But we still don't know where she is!" Tears filled her eyes and this time she couldn't hold them back.

Sinking onto the sofa next to her mother, she buried her face in her hands and sobbed. Warm arms enfolded her and she let her mother hold her as they shared their common fear in a flood of tears.

A hand covered the back of her head and soft whispers finally reached her ears.

Her father was praying.

But would God hear this man? She thought He might now. In the short time she'd been home, he'd proven to be a different person than the one she grew up with. Her mother had told her he was, and Lacey had to admit she had seen a huge difference in the man ever since they'd moved in.

She looked up and palmed the tears from her cheeks. Her mother did the same, and her father returned to his recliner, leaned his head back and closed his eyes.

But his lips still moved. Her heart breaking at their anguish, she sighed and headed for the kitchen.

Her mother hurried after her, wiping her own tears on a tissue magically produced from one o

er pockets. "What is it, Lacey? What are you
ot telling us?"

Lacey pulled the milk from the fridge and the
ocoa, sugar and other items from the cabinet.
"Want some hot chocolate?" So what if it was
ighty-five degrees outside. She felt chilled from
he inside out.

Her mother watched her, sighed and pulled two
mugs from the cupboard. "Sure, that would be
ovely."

"Bethany loves this stuff," Lacey murmured.
"She always has. I never could fool her when I
ixed the package mix. She would always shake
er head and say I fixed her the fake chocolate
nd she wanted the real deal."

"She's turned into a wonderful girl, Lacey," her
mother said softly. "You've done a magnificent
ob. And all by yourself, too."

Lacey watched her mom purse her lips and
blink back tears. "Well, I did have a little help.
God placed some amazing people in my path
along the way."

She wondered whether or not to broach the
question she'd wanted to ask for years. Then went
or it. "What did the congregation say when I basi-
ally disappeared that summer, never to be seen
rom again?"

Her mother drew in a deep breath. "Oh, my.

That was one of the hardest summers of my life."

Surprised, Lacey froze then turned to look at her. "Why?"

"Why?" Her mother gave an incredulous laugh that held no humor. "Because I had to send my baby girl away." Tears filled her eyes and she looked away. "I didn't want to but your father convinced me it was for the best."

"He had an image to maintain," Lacey said angrily. She couldn't help it. The words came out wrapped in hurt and bitterness.

A resigned sigh filtered from her mother. "Yes, there was that. But it was more. He felt like you betrayed him—us—and everything that we taught you. He felt like you betrayed yourself." Her mother shrugged and swiped a few more stray tears.

"Well," Lacey admitted, "I suppose I did, but I think the punishment didn't really fit the crime."

"I agree."

"So what did the church say?" Her mother had avoided answering that one.

The woman sighed. "Your father told them you'd decided to go to school in North Carolina."

"Hmm. The truth. At least part of it."

"Yes. Of course it was the truth. He would never lie, you know." Surprised, Lacey wondered if she idn't detect a hint of bitterness in her mother's oice. With a start, she realized her mother had er own regrets. She poured the milk into the aucepan and turned on the stove. "Knowing what you know now, would you have done things ifferently?"

Her mother looked her in the eye. "In a heart-eat."

Lacey expected to feel satisfaction, a surge of ictory that she'd managed to make her mom egret sending her away. Instead she just felt sad or all the missed years, missed family time, and ne missed granddaughter/grandparent time Beth-ny should have experienced growing up.

On impulse, she threw her arms around her nom and gave her a hug. "I'm sorry," she said. I'm sorry I was so stubborn and unforgiving. I'm orry I waited so long to come home and share 3ethany with you."

Her mother's arms enclosed her in that embrace he remembered from childhood. "I know. I'm orry, too." When she pulled back, she cupped acey's face and said, "But let's not think about vhat we missed. Let's think about what we have n front of us. A lifetime of love." She tightened er lips. "As soon as we get Bethany back."

"Deal. It's not going to be about what was nissed. It's going to be about the future."

Her mother patted her arm. "I've got to get you father's medication for him."

Lacey rubbed her bleary eyes. "I'm going to li down for a few minutes."

With one last hug, the two parted and Lacey started down the hall to her bedroom with he mug.

Settling on the bed, she pulled her laptop towar her. Might as well work while she could. Just a she powered up the machine, a knock on her doo sounded.

"Come in."

The door swung open and her father entered.

Surprised, she could only stare at him with on brow raised. He rarely sought her out since she' been home. "Hey."

"Hi." He looked uneasy as he stood in the entrance.

Taking pity on him, she motioned him inside "What is it?"

Blowing out a sigh, he raised one hand to rul his balding head. "I have something I need to tel you and it's going to be one of the hardest thing I've ever done." He glanced at her from the corne of his eye. "I'm working up my nerve."

Puzzled, she simply looked at him.

"All right," he said, moving to the chair by the small desk on the opposite wall. "I guess there' nothing to it but to come out and say it."

She waited.

Clearing his throat, her father said, "I was wrong. And prideful."

She drew in a deep breath. "About?"

"Sending you away." Looking down at his hands, she saw his fingers work and wring themselves together. Finally, his head lifted and he swallowed again. "The night you came to us and told us you were pregnant was surreal to me. I remember it in a haze—and with such disappointment and—anger."

She really didn't need this right now. "Dad…"

He held up a hand. "Just let me finish, please."

Wilting back against the pillow, she conceded.

Her father rubbed his mouth then shook his head. "I had just counseled a father that day. His daughter was seventeen years old and had told her parents that she was pregnant. In my… stupidity…I essentially blamed him. Told him what a bad father he'd been and how the teachings of his household and his spiritual leadership had obviously fallen short. In a word, I judged him lacking."

"Because his daughter got pregnant," Lacey said dully.

"Yes."

It all became startling clear. "I see now."

"I'm sure you do."

Tears formed in his tired eyes, and Lacey force
herself not to look away. Instead, she said, "S
when I told you I was pregnant…"

He gave a short, humorless laugh. "Don't thin
the irony escaped me."

Her throat ached with the effort to hold back he
tears. "And you certainly couldn't have me sho
up in church, pregnant."

"No, my pride wouldn't have that." He sighe
and looked away. "So, the only option availab
was to send you away."

Old hurt welled up inside her. She forced
away. The time had come to forgive. It was th
reason she had come home in the first place
And what he was saying was nothing she hadn
thought about. She knew his sending her awa
had to do with his pride, she just hadn't realize
how much. Only now, he sat before her a humb
and broken man.

Rising from the bed she pushed the laptop asid
and walked to her father's side. Kneeling besid
him, she took his hand in hers. "I forgive you
Dad."

A sob escaped him. "How?" he whispered.

"Because God forgave me."

He knew what she meant. In one move, he gath
ered her to his thin, shaking frame and buried hi

ace in her hair. "Thank you, Lacey. I know I don't deserve it."

"I don't, either."

He pulled back. "Can we move on from here?"

Lacey stood, her knees popping. She gave a shaky laugh. "I think moving on from here's going o be the easy part—as soon as we get Bethany home."

Her father stood, too, and stroked her cheek. "You're a fabulous mother. You've done a wonderful job with her."

Tears threatened once again but she choked them down. "Thanks, Dad."

With one last hug, he walked from her room.

Which left Lacey staring across the hall at another closed door.

Bethany's.

On impulse, she took a deep breath, walked to it and put her hand on the knob. She closed her eyes and opened Bethany's door. Slowly, she opened her eyes and breathed a sigh of relief when nothing seemed out of the ordinary.

The mess from the other night had been cleaned up. She shuddered at the memory and tried not to visualize Bethany's features over that of the wig holder.

Lacey's mother had washed and dried the bed-

spread and all was as it should be. Waiting fo
Bethany to return to her rightful place.

Oh, Bethany, where are you, darling?

Lacey sat on Bethany's bed and picked up he
pillow. Breathing in, she realized that the washin
had taken away most of Bethany's scent.

Hurrying to the closet, she opened the doo
and pulled up short. A strange faint smell greete
her. A smell that seemed familiar yet she couldn'
place it. It wasn't Bethany, that much she knew.

Unless Bethany had changed perfumes.

A chill swept over her. How had a strange—
yet familiar—scent gotten in here? Had someon
been in this closet? And when?

Quickly, she took inventory. Unlike most teen
agers, Bethany didn't have a closet full of clothes
Lacey hadn't been able to afford them, not i
Bethany wanted to keep up with the karate. Fo
a long time, it had been hand-to-mouth, paycheck
to-paycheck living. All of Bethany's clothes wer
accounted for except for the ones she was wearin
when she'd disappeared.

Except for her purple A-shaped shirt with the
ruffled collar and a pair of jeans.

Why hadn't she noticed this before? She'd gon
through Bethany's clothes when her mother ha
voiced concerns that Bethany had left willingly.

All of her clothes had been there at that time.

Including the shirt and jeans.

So when had these disappeared?

Last night when the person after her had been in her house? And why?

Because the person felt that Bethany needed a change of clothes? Maybe?

Again, why?

Lacey shuddered. Felt the hair on her neck stand straight up. This was so wrong.

She fingered the rest of the clothes. All accounted for. Moving from the closet to Bethany's dresser, she opened the top drawer.

All looked undisturbed. Socks, underwear… Lacey's diary.

Her breath whooshed out and she opened the book.

April 1st
Today MS kissed me for the first time. I laughed, I couldn't help it. He was so cute and so nervous…and so gallant. I didn't laugh too much, though. I can't believe he waited a whole month of dating before kissing me. He's so incredibly wonderful. I can't wait to see where all this goes.
April 16th
MS told me that his mother left his father a couple of years ago. That she had a lot of affairs and lied to his dad about all of them. And his dad believed her. MS was

so disgusted with her. I'm surprised he's even interested in dating after watching his parents' marriage fall apart. I want to do everything in my power to prove to him that I'll always be there for him. I know he'd be there for me—through anything. I love him so much.

Lacey slapped the book closed. She couldn't relive that right now. Replacing the diary back where she'd gotten it from, she decided to let Bethany decide when to approach her about it.

Closing the drawer, she thought about Mason confronting Daniel. She wondered what Daniel would say. Would he finally admit his big lie after all these years? Or would he continue to deny it?

Lacey swallowed hard and decided she didn't care as long as Mason believed her. That was all she'd wanted for as long as she could remember.

She opened the next drawer. Scarves, belts, jogging shorts and T-shirts. Again, nothing out of place.

Wait a minute. Lacey picked up one of the scarves and flashed to the memory of Daniel finding the one at the scene.

The place Bethany had disappeared from.

The place where someone had dropped a scarf?

Raising the item to her nose, she inhaled. It smelled like Bethany.

But reminded her of someone else.

Someone who might be Bethany's kidnapper.

EIGHTEEN

Mason had just pulled into the police station parking lot when his cell phone rang.

Joseph.

"Hello?"

"Hey, Mason. I just heard back from my contact at the lab."

"What have you got?"

"For one, the print on the car is a match with our Mr. Howe."

Satisfaction curled in Mason. Then fizzled. So far, having Howe in custody hadn't helped Bethany. "So, who's he working with? We need a name."

"On the advice of his lawyer, Howe has decided not to say anything further at this time." Joseph sounded disgusted. Mason could relate.

"Great." He sighed. "I wonder if Daniel questioned that other person from the shelter that Troy mentioned."

"He said he was going to."

"I'll give him a call in a minute."

He climbed out of his car as he said, "Okay, so what can they charge Howe with?"

"Attempted kidnapping, obstruction, leaving the scene of an accident. Just for starters."

"Good. What about the white Buick?"

"Excuse me?"

"Daniel said he asked Catelyn to get a list of all of the white Buicks listed within a thirty-mile radius of the city. He seemed to think she was going to pass that on to you because you could get the information faster."

A pause. "I haven't heard from Daniel, and Catelyn hasn't said a word to me about a white Buick."

Mason pictured Daniel at the crime scene. He'd seemed tense. Anxious. Why?

Unbidden, the memory of Lacey practically accusing Daniel of being the one after her came to mind. Daniel wouldn't cover something up, would he? Like maybe the fact that he really was the one after Lacey?

Mason seriously didn't like the directions his thoughts were taking. "Okay." Very strange. "Before Bethany disappeared on us again, she said a white Buick always seemed to be in the area. She was afraid of whoever was in it. While she was on the phone with me, she spotted it again."

Joseph grunted. "I'll have that list for you ASAP."

"Great. Anything else?"

"Not yet. I'll be in touch."

His phone beeped, indicating he had another call coming in. "Hey, Lacey's on the other line. I'll talk to you soon."

Mason switched over. "Hi, Lacey."

"Mason, where are you?"

"At the station. Where are you?" His voice sharpened. "You didn't leave the house unprotected again did you?"

"Yes, I'm on the way to the station. I want to see that piece of material that was found at the scene."

"Material? What material?"

"The material Daniel picked up and bagged for evidence. I've seen it somewhere before and now I want to smell it."

The pressure had been too much. She'd finally snapped. Lost it. "Lacey, darling..."

"I'm not crazy. I'm almost there. Can you meet me and get me in to see the evidence?"

He thought about it. Catelyn wouldn't have a problem with him seeing it. And if Lacey thought it would help find Bethany, Catelyn would be open to that, too. "I see you turning in the parking lot."

She pulled in beside him and his heart did that

unny thing whenever she was around. He swallowed hard and pushed aside surging feelings.

Soon he would be able to act on those feelings. As soon as they found Bethany. They were getting close, he could feel it.

Lacey bolted from her car and headed for the door, leaving him to bring up the rear. "Hey, Lacey, you want to wait on me?"

She shot him an apologetic look but didn't stop her rush. "I need to see that scrap of material."

"There was no scrap of material."

The look she gave him said she thought he was dense. "Yes, there was. I saw him pick it up and put it in a brown paper bag."

He sighed. "All right, come on, let's go look at the evidence log."

Together they entered the building and Mason kept up with Lacey by lengthening his stride to match her short, quick steps.

Lacey screeched to a stop as she nearly collided with Catelyn who'd rounded the corner in front of her. "Catelyn. Just the person I wanted to see."

Catelyn looked back and forth between them. "What is it?"

Mason stepped forward and placed a calming hand on Lacey's shoulder. She shifted, impatient, but let him take the lead. "Could we see the evidence log on this afternoon's incident in front of the homeless shelter?"

Tilting her head, Catelyn studied him. "Sure."

She led the way down the hall. Stopping at he office, she motioned them inside. "Wait here."

Ten minutes later, she returned with a piece o paper. "Here you go."

Mason took the paper from her and felt Lace crowd in next to him.

He didn't mind one bit.

Holding the paper so she could see it, he scanne the log. Then he looked at Lacey. "There's n piece of material listed here."

"What?" she cried, and snatched the paper fror his hand. She perused it, her finger running ove each item. "I don't understand." She looked up frustration glittering in her green eyes. "I watche him pick it up and put it in a brown paper bag."

"Did he say it was evidence?"

That seemed to stump her. She shook her head "No, not exactly. I think he even said something like it wasn't much of anything. But he said he' have them check it out, anyway. He told that t the cop who was standing next to him."

"Do you know which cop?"

Lacey sighed and bit her lip. "No. I don' remember his name. He was tall, thin and prett young. Like maybe in his mid-twenties?"

Mason pursed his lips. She'd just described fift percent of the police force. Through various meth

ds, he could find the guy, but it would take time.
Time Bethany might not have.

Lacey's fingers curled into fists by her side. "I
know there was a scrap of material and it's impor-
ant." She stared at Mason. "I was in Bethany's
closet a little while ago. She's missing a shirt and
a pair of jeans. They weren't missing before that
thing appeared on her bed. I think the person hid
out in the closet—" her voice wobbled "—and
was there when I found that…thing. The smell in
he closet reminds me of…" She broke off and bit
her lip.

"Who, Lacey?"

"Daniel," she whispered. At Catelyn's shocked
look, she gave a small shrug. "I'm sorry."

Mason rubbed his nose. "All right. Let's just
call Daniel and ask him about it."

Although this information, along with the fact
that Daniel hadn't asked Catelyn about the white
Buick, fueled his suspicions. And it hurt. And
made him feel like an idiot. All this time he'd
believed a lie. And Daniel had been playing him
for a fool. Secretly laughing that he'd managed to
come between Lacey and Mason.

But why?

Because he'd wanted her for himself. How could
he have been so blind? A memory surfaced. Specifically, Daniel's comments about Mason being
a lucky guy to have a girl like Lacey. One time,

Lacey had been cheering at a football game
Mason had caught Daniel watching her so closely
that it made Mason uncomfortable. He'd asked
"You got something you need to tell me?"

Daniel had jerked and said, "No, why?"

"Because you're eyeing Lacey like a lion on a
hunt."

Daniel had simply peered at him through narrowed eyes, then shrugged. "Just thinking how
you always seem to get what you want. I'm no
sure I think that's fair."

Mason had laughed. "Yeah, I know. Maybe one
day ya'll grow up to be like me."

Mason blinked as the memory zipped through
him at warp speed. And he knew.

Cold, hard certainty settled like a rock in the
pit of his stomach as he pulled his phone from the
clip. Daniel was behind all this.

"But what about the piece of material? It could
have been the scarf. In fact, the more I think abou
it the more I'm sure it is. Definitely a scarf," Lacey
said.

He frowned and his finger hesitated above the
button that would send the call. "The material you
think Daniel hid?"

"Yes." She flushed but didn't back down. "Who
could it belong to? The woman who helped Bethany?" She sucked in a breath as a horrible thought
hit her. "If he's the one who has Bethany, tha

carf—or whatever it was—could lead him to the woman who helped her! No wonder he hid it. He wants to be the one to find her so he can silence her for good!"

Doubtful, but… "Possibly."

Catelyn spoke up. "I checked all the hospitals. No one reported seeing anyone by Bethany's description being brought in."

Mason nodded. "And we didn't get a good description of the woman who supposedly helped Bethany. All right," he said, narrowing his eyes. "Let's track down Daniel and question him." He punched Daniel's number in his cell phone and waited.

Nothing.

He looked at Catelyn. "You have any idea why he wouldn't be answering his cell?"

Catelyn looked uneasy. "No. I don't like that. You know as well as I do, an on-duty cop is always a phone call away. He should be answering."

"Sometimes he forgets to turn it on Ring, remember?" Lacey reminded them. "Janice fussed at him about it a couple of days ago."

"Right. Then I suppose we can drive around until we spot him."

"We'll try him on his car radio, too," Catelyn suggested. "Put out over the air that we're looking for him and would he please call in."

"Good." Mason looked at Lacey. "You sit tight and wait here."

"But…"

"No buts." He pointed a finger at her. "And I mean it."

She sighed. "Okay." What was she going to do anyway? She had no clue who the woman was who was seen helping Bethany and she couldn't track down Daniel. "Fine."

But she could be here when they got back with him.

Lacey watched them leave and paced, feeling like she'd lived this scene once before.

Thinking that Daniel hated her enough to cause her this much grief shook her. Always she'd been kind to him. Back in high school, she'd been aware that he'd had a crush on her, but she didn't push him away. She did her best to keep everything on a friendship level and it had seemed to work.

At least until she started dating Mason.

At first, he seemed to take it in stride. Then over time, his attitude toward her changed. Slowly, almost imperceptibly. When she realized she didn't want to be around him, she started finding excuses why she and Mason should do things alone.

Because even though Daniel had been in love with her, he'd still dated. Nothing serious and nothing that ever lasted. She didn't want to be foursome. She got tired of Daniel's ugly looks and snide comments when no one was around to hear.

And Janice. Dear sweet Janice had been crazy about Daniel since the sixth grade. And he never gave her a second look. Not even in high school. Nothing she'd done had ever gotten his attention.

Not her makeovers, her clothes, her…

Clothes.

Scarves.

"That's it!" she said aloud. "That scarf—" and she felt sure that's what it was "—belongs to Janice!"

Had Janice been the woman who'd rescued Bethany? But if she had, why hadn't she brought her home? And how had she known where Bethany was going to be?

Unless she'd found out what Daniel was up to and acted.

And she'd never met Bethany, so she wouldn't know who the girl was. But she'd seen her picture from the flyer. Then again, after living on the street this long, Bethany probably didn't look anything like her flyer picture. What if she'd disguised herself somehow?

And if Bethany had been injected with something, she could be unconscious and unable to tell Janice anything.

A hard fist formed in her stomach. She reached across the desk and grabbed the phone. She dialed Mason's cell phone and it rang several times before going to voice mail.

He was probably on the phone trying to get ahold of Daniel. At the tone, she said, "I think know who helped Bethany. That scarf is Janice's. I think Daniel was in the closet that night because her perfume is so strong, it was on his clothes. That's why it lingered. I'm going to see if I can find Janice. I have my cell phone."

Hanging up, she wondered if she should try Catelyn's phone. But she didn't have the number and didn't want to take the time to look it up. Mason would get the message and pass it on.

She hurried from the office and down to the parking lot—where once again, she didn't have a car.

Growling, she pulled out her cell phone and dialed Janice's home number. She felt sure if she found Janice, she would find Bethany.

No answer.

She dialed the woman's cell phone.

No answer.

Frustrated, she thought.

The store!

Hurrying back inside, she asked the desk sergeant to look the number up for her. He did and she dialed it.

Again, no answer.

Wanting to weep with frustration, she bolted out to grab the nearest taxi. Climbing in, she gave the driver the address to Janice's home and prayed aloud, "Please, Lord, lead me to my child. Please let her be okay."

The driver simply glanced in the rearview mirror.

The ten-minute drive to the Ackerman's house seemed to take forever. Tempted to urge the man to speed, she held on to her self-control. She couldn't afford the time it would take for the cop to write him a ticket.

When the taxi pulled into the driveway, she hopped out. "Wait here, please." She didn't want him driving off if Janice wasn't there. She ran to the front door.

Banging on it brought no results. No one was home. Groaning, she ran back to the taxi and told him to just wait a minute while she thought.

He did.

She checked her cell phone to see if Mason had called. He hadn't.

The next logical place to go was Janice's store. Mind made up, she gave the driver the address.

When Lacey arrived, her heart dropped to her toes once again. This place also looked deserted. She frowned and bit her lip. What should she do?

Climbing from the vehicle with another request that he wait, she approached the front door, absently noticing the greenery entwined around the white-painted stair rails. Green wreaths with red bows hung on the double wooden doors. An Opening Soon sign hung from a nail at eye level.

Lacey knocked.

And waited. Nothing.

Great. Now what?

A crash from inside made her gasp.

She banged on the door. "Janice? Janice? Are you in there? Are you all right?"

A muffled scream?

"Janice!" Lacey twisted the doorknob and the door flew open.

NINETEEN

Mason finally got Daniel on the phone. Just as Daniel answered, he heard the call-waiting signal. Lacey. She would have to wait. To Daniel, he said, "We need to talk, Ackerman." It was all he could do to keep the fury out of his voice. This man had lied to him all these years, terrorized Lacey and kidnapped Bethany.

"Sorry, I was working an accident out on the highway, then just now finished questioning a suspect in Bethany's kidnapping. Billy Rose admitted that someone paid him to watch for her and inject her."

Was this guy for real?

"Did he happen to say who that someone was?"

"No, he didn't."

"Of course not."

"Look—" Daniel cleared his throat "—we need to talk. Where are you?"

"About ten minutes away from the station. Cate lyn's with me."

"Meet me in the parking lot at the corner of Henry and Pine."

"I'm on the way and you'd better be there."

Mason hung up and looked at Catelyn. He said "I'm confused. Your partner is not acting like a guilty man."

"He wants to meet?"

"Yeah, he said we needed to talk."

"What if it's a trap? Should I call for back-up?"

Mason nodded. "It sure wouldn't hurt. But tel them to stay out of sight unless we need them."

A few minutes later, Mason pulled into the parking lot specified by Daniel and saw the man's unmarked car parked in the corner. Rolling to a stop beside him, Mason rolled down his window "Where's Bethany?"

Confusion and a small flicker of fear crossed Daniel's face. "I don't know, but I'm afraid I might know who does."

Mason tensed and Catelyn shifted beside him. "What do you mean, Daniel?"

"I, uh, found some evidence that points to—" he closed his eyes and took a deep breath "—Janice."

"What?" Catelyn exclaimed. "Why would you say that?"

"Does this have anything to do with the scarf you found?"

A flush covered the man's cheeks. "How did you know about that?"

"Lacey saw you put it in a bag. She wanted to check out the evidence for some reason and it wasn't listed on the evidence log."

A muscle jumped in his cheek. "I know. I was wrong. I should have logged it, but it caught me completely by surprise. I honestly convinced myself that it was a fluke."

"What changed your mind?"

"Billy's testimony."

"Which was?"

"He said a woman paid him five hundred dollars to inject that fluid into a girl." He paused and cleared his throat. "He also said the woman drove off in a white Buick."

"Let me guess, Janice drives a white Buick."

Misery on his face, Daniel nodded. "Sometimes. It's her father's car. For some reason she likes to drive it and will go trade her car out for it."

She likes to drive it so no one can connect her to anything she's doing, Mason thought. He looked at Catelyn, "Excuse me for a minute."

He motioned Daniel to talk in private. With a resigned look, he followed Daniel to the other side of the car so they could talk without being overheard.

Mason got right to it. "Just tell me. You lied to me about Lacey, didn't you?"

Shame flashed across Daniel's face and then his jaw hardened. "Yeah. I did."

The words punched the breath from his lungs. "Why?" he finally managed.

Daniel's eyes narrowed and something close to hate entered them. "Because it was always so easy for you. Everything you touched turned to gold. I was sick of it."

"So you wrecked three people's lives as a result?"

The man shook his head. "I can't explain it, Mason. I'm not proud of it, but I did it."

Before he could come back with a response, Mason's cell buzzed, indicating he'd missed a call. He looked at the number. Lacey.

Dialing his voice mail, he indicated to Catelyn he needed to listen. She nodded.

Lacey's voice came on the line. "I think I know who helped Bethany. That scarf is Janice's. I think Daniel was in the closet that night because her perfume is so strong, it was on his clothes. That's why it lingered. I'm going to see if I can find Janice. I have my cell phone."

Mason felt the bottom drop out of his stomach. Lacey was walking into the hands of a possible killer.

* * *

Lacey gaped at the woman standing before her. Janice looked—ruffled. Her hair stood on end and sweat dripped from her chin.

"Janice! Are you all right?"

Janice pulled a tissue from her pocket and wiped at her forehead, smearing the makeup and leaving a white streak behind. She tossed it into the trashcan beside the door. "No, not really."

"What's wrong?"

"Nothing. Everything." Frustrated tears appeared in Janice's eyes and Lacey's heart went out to her. But first things first.

"Is Bethany here with you?"

Janice blinked in confusion. "Bethany? No."

Lacey groaned. "Then you weren't the woman who helped her?"

She broke off as Janice turned mid-question to head to the back of the store. "I need to clean that up," she muttered.

"Janice…"

"Sorry, can you help me? It's in the back room."

"What is?"

"What I need help with."

The sudden calm in Janice's voice disturbed Lacey. When Lacey turned to look at her, the woman slipped around her and disappeared into the back.

The hair on the back of Lacey's neck stood attention. Something didn't feel right.

But she had to warn Janice about Daniel. A ask Janice about Bethany again.

As she stepped through the door to follo Janice, the darkness hit her. "Janice, do you ha some light back here?"

"Yes, sorry," Janice called. "I'm looking for t switch."

But then Lacey saw a sliver of light just ahe and made a beeline for it. She blamed her jum ness on the darkness.

And then her phone vibrated.

She snatched it from her purse and looked the caller ID.

Mason. She owed it to him to answer and him know she'd found Bethany.

She pressed the button to answer the call wh she felt something press into the middle of h back.

"What...?"

"Just stay right there," a voice hissed into h ear.

She froze. "Janice? What are you doing?"

"What needed to be done years ago."

Was that a gun the woman had jammed in her spine? Chills shivered over her and she felt wave of sickness claim her.

Shaking it off, she stood still. "Janice?"

"Shut up and move straight ahead."

Swallowing, Lacey placed the phone into her
ɪrse praying Mason was on the other end.

Terror invaded Mason as he listened to the
enace in Janice's voice. She wasn't playing
ound. He motioned for Catelyn to be quiet as
ɪe drove, not wanting to miss one detail as to
hat was going on with Lacey and Janice. Where
ere they?

Come on, honey, give me a clue.

Twisting, he looked at Daniel in the backseat
ɪd whispered, "Where would Janice be this time
` day?"

Daniel threw his hands up and shrugged. "I
ɪn't know. The hospital maybe." He grimaced.
No, that's on Friday. The clothes closet at the
ɪurch? Um…no! Try the store."

Mason glared at the man. "Give her directions."

While Daniel leaned forward to whisper in
atelyn's left ear, Mason listened.

"Why are you doing this?" Lacey's fear came
ɪrough loud and clear in her shaky voice.
ɪason wanted to reach through the phone line
ɪd wrap his hands around Janice's neck.

But he couldn't. All he could do was pray.

* * *

Lacey walked into the lighted area and her ga
landed on a thin figure stretched out on a flim
cot in the corner of the room.

"Bethany!" With a small cry, Lacey launche
herself at her child.

Bethany lay on a cot, hands bound behind he
duct tape covering her mouth. Her eyes opene
and closed as though trying to wake up.

"Bethany," Lacey whispered.

At her name, Bethany's eyes flickered again

Lacey placed her palms on her daughter
cheeks and felt her warmth, her life. *Thank yo
Jesus.* She ripped the tape from Bethany's mou
and the girl gasped, opened her eyes. "Mom," sl
whispered.

"Okay, enough of that," Janice ordered. "Mo
over there and sit down."

"No, I'm not leaving her." Lacey took in eve
detail of her precious child. She was dressed in tl
clothes that Lacey had discovered missing fro
Bethany's closet. Reddish-blond hair that looke
more brown than it ever had lay in a hunk ov
one shoulder. Her foggy blue eyes wouldn't foc
and her light dusting of freckles stood out in 3-
against pale white cheeks. "What did you gi
her?"

"A fast-acting narcotic. Nothing she wor
recover from. Although—" Janice's eyes narrowe

—she'll only recover long enough for you to
atch her die."

Terror slid through Lacey once more as she
ared at the woman who used to be her best
iend. "Why, Janice? What did I do to you to
ake you hate me? Hate my child? To want us
ead?"

"Why?" Janice screamed at her. "What did
u do? Everything! It's all your fault! All of
!" Lacey watched Janice gather herself with an
ffort. The woman pulled in a deep breath and
aved the gun at Bethany. "You don't deserve
er. You should never have been allowed to have
er and watch her grow up." Evil stared back at
acey and she shivered at the cold emptiness that
ad seemed to have invaded Janice's soul.

Lacey held up a hand, beseeching her, "I don't
nderstand. We were friends. Best friends. We
id everything together. And now you hate me?
doesn't make sense."

In slow, measured words, Janice spat, "Because
aniel always loved you. It was always about
u."

"What? That's not true. He *married* you!"

"But he never loved me! Not like he loved you!
ven after we were married, he would get this
raway look on his face and I'd ask him what he
as thinking about and he'd shrug and say 'Old

times.'" She snarled, "Well, we all know who wa in those old times, don't we?"

"Janice, I can't…I don't…" What could she say What *should* she say to convince Janice to l them go? "I was gone! I wasn't here. How ca you hold me responsible for that?"

It didn't seem possible, but Janice's eyes gre harder and the gun jabbed at Lacey. "Because yo killed my baby."

Bethany whimpered and shrank back again the wall, but didn't say a word.

Shock made her Lacey gasp. "What? How that possible? You said you lost the baby when yo fell down the steps." Was the woman complete insane?

Looking into those eyes, Lacey had a feelin she had her answer. And it terrified her.

"You want to know why I lost the baby? D you?" Janice hissed as she waved the gun in wild gesture. "Because you exist!"

Bethany's eyes, looking a lot less foggy no that some of the medication was wearing off, sh back and forth between her kidnapper and h mother.

Janice screamed again. "And then you had th nerve to come back!"

With a sinking heart, Lacey realized she wasr

oing to be able to reason with the woman, and
ocused on trying to figure out how to disarm
er.

But Janice said, "I found him looking at your
ictures. The ones in the yearbook."

Confused, Lacey just kept her mouth shut.

"Oh, yes," Janice continued. "I found him. Six
ears ago, sitting on the sofa around Christmas-
me. He was looking at the yearbook. I asked
im what he was doing and he just shrugged and
napped the book shut. I sat down next to him
or a trip down memory lane, but—" she wagged
finger "—memory lane didn't have anything
o do with me. It was all about you!" The finger
bbed in Lacey's direction and spittle flew from
er mouth.

Lacey felt compassion mix with her fear.

Janice paced the floor, the pain on her face
orrible to see. "I was so mad, *hurt.* Here I was,
nally pregnant with his child and he was looking
t pictures of *you.*"

"Oh, Janice, I'm so sorry."

"You should be!" The gun waved wildly and
acey cringed.

"But I wasn't there," she stated softly. "I didn't
ave anything to do with that. I didn't have any
ontrol over that."

"You weren't there?" Janice gave a laugh filled

with disbelief. "Oh you were there, all right. Yo
were everywhere. In the church, in the grocer
store, in my own house!" She mocked, "Thos
are pretty flowers. I think they were Lacey'
favorite."

Oh, Daniel, what did you do? Lord, please...

"I was never interested in Daniel, Janice. Yo
know that! How many times did I say how muc
I wished he'd just leave me alone?"

"That's what you said." Janice sneered. "Bu
you never did anything to discourage him. Yo
just kept letting him hang around you. And yo
loved it. All the attention you were getting fron
two of the best-looking guys in school. Don't den
you ate it up."

"I did not!" Lacey protested, but for a brie
moment, a little piece of her mind questione
whether or not Janice was right. She sputtere
"But he was Mason's best friend and I didn't wan
to hurt his feelings."

Skepticism twisted Janice's features. "Right.
She stepped closer and shoved the gun at Bethan
who flinched and gave a cry. Lacey held up a han
in supplication. "Don't! She's never done anythin
to you."

"No, she didn't," Janice said, her suddenly cal
tone sending darts of terror through Lacey. "Sh
didn't, but her mother did. Because of you, I ra
out of the house seven months pregnant, intendin

get in the car and go to a motel. But do you now what happened? Do you?"

Lacey refused to cringe. She had a pretty good ea of what Janice was getting ready to say and anted to tell her to stop. She didn't want to hear

But she couldn't. Janice had to say it. And if e stopped talking, she might start shooting.

Vhat?" Lacey whispered.

"I fell. I slipped on the stupid ice my husband dn't scrape off the steps and I nearly bled to eath at the bottom of my front porch." Janice ded the sentence on a whisper. She raised the in and pointed it at Bethany's head. "And it's all our fault. You, who had a perfect little girl after lling mine."

"No, Janice, don't do this, please."

TWENTY

Mason felt his heart beat in a way that threatened to punch a hole in his shirt. Hand wrapped around his gun, he started for the door as soon as Catelyn pulled to a stop. Daniel simply sat in the backseat defeated as his wife's words sunk in.

At the door, he felt a hand on his arm. "You're too close to this. You need to hang back."

Mason hardened his jaw. "No way."

"If you jeopardize this in any way, you could get them killed."

He stared at her, her words impacting him. "I won't," he promised. "Professional all the way."

Catelyn drew in a deep breath and nodded. "Fine."

Mason had never told Catelyn that Bethany was his daughter. She must have figured it out. Either that or he didn't hide his feelings for Lacey very well, and she'd realized he was in love with Lacey.

It didn't matter, he was going in.

Daniel said Janice had an alarm on the doors leading in through the front. A SWAT team was on standby. From listening in on the conversation between Janice and Lacey, Mason knew they were in the back of the store.

That door didn't have an alarm, but according to Daniel would be visible from where he suspected Janice would be.

Catelyn had snagged him an extra earpiece. He shoved it in deeper and listened closely. Lacey still had her phone on.

From what he could tell, Janice had the gun on Bethany and planned to kill her.

At the back door three SWAT members held the battering ram. On the count of three, they'd ram it down.

One.

Two.

Three.

A loud crash sounded and Mason rounded the doorway with Catelyn. "Freeze! Police!" she shouted.

Mason took in the scene in a split second. Janice, her back to the front of the store, held the gun to Bethany's head.

Bethany had her eyes closed and Lacey looked frozen, eyes wide on the action before her. "Mason," she whispered.

He held up a hand to tell her to be still.

She didn't move.

Catelyn stared down the barrel of the gun sh
now had trained on Janice. "Ma'am, I need yo
to please put that gun down."

Fury lit in Janice's eyes. "Why? How…"

A low beeping came from the direction c
Lacey's purse and she jerked. Janice screeched
"What is that? What is that?"

Lacey reached in her purse and pulled out he
cell phone in a slow, methodical manner. "Dea
battery," she monotoned. Then blinked an
seemed to gather her wits. "Please, Janice, I'll d
anything you want, just let Bethany go."

The woman sneered and jabbed the gun harde
against Bethany's head. The teen winced and ange
twisted in Mason's gut. Soothing his voice so n
hint of ire or emotion showed, he said, "Janice
there's nothing you can do now except give up
Just set the gun down and no one has to get hur
right?"

"I've already been hurt. I've been hurt so muc
I don't think I know what it feels like not to hu
anymore." Her brow crinkled. "Where's Daniel?
she asked suddenly.

"We wouldn't let him come in," Mason answere
immediately. "Protocol, you know. There's no wa
he'd be allowed to come in."

"Liar!" she screamed at him. "I want him here. want him to see what he's done. Get him in ere."

Catelyn held up a hand. "Calm down, Mrs. Ack-rman, Janice. I'll get him to come talk to you if at'll help."

"Oh, it'll help. I have a few things I want to say efore all this is over."

Mason blew out a breath and watched Catelyn et Daniel on the phone.

Lacey couldn't seem to take her eyes from Bethany's scared face. Her breathing seemed abored, but Lacey decided it was just from the ear. She didn't seem to be having any negative ide effects to whatever drug had been injected nto her system.

"Where'd you get the drug?" Mason asked onversationally.

Janice smirked. "I volunteer at the hospital, emember. I have access to a lot of places. And o one even looks twice at me. Now shut up, I ave to think." She looked at Mason, Catelyn and Lacey and blinked. Her breath started coming in ants.

"What drug did you use?" Lacey needed the nformation. When she got Bethany out of here, he needed to be able to tell the doctor what was njected in her.

Janice shifted, pulled in a deep breath and rolle her eyes. "Ketamine. It's used in surgeries. All had to do was sneak in the operating room afte hours and snatch it from the cart."

The cart that held the medications used in su gery. Easily accessible to someone who knew he way around the hospital and where the drugs wer kept.

Lacey shifted toward Bethany who seemed t be more conscious and taking it all in. Her eye never stopped, bouncing between her mother an the woman with the gun. Then her eyes fixed o Mason and she frowned.

A phone rang and Janice jerked, her finge twitching on the trigger. Lacey flinched, expec ing to hear the sharp crack of the gun.

It didn't happen and she breathed a prayer c thanks. The phone rang again.

"That's Daniel," Catelyn offered.

Indecision flickered over Janice's face, then sh said to Lacey. "Answer it."

Lacey reached out a shaky hand to snatcl the cordless handset from the wall. She held out to Janice who snapped, "Put it on speake phone."

Lacey pressed the button and Janice said, "S you had the guts to call."

"They said you wanted to talk to me."

* * *

Mason's gut clenched and twisted on top of self as Daniel's terse voice came over the phone. Mason had a hard time restraining himself from throwing his body at the woman who had a gun trained on his daughter's head. But he promised. As Bethany's eyes stared at him, questions flickered there and he gave her a slow wink.

She blinked and tears sprang to her eyes. "Daddy," she whispered, her voice almost no more than a whisper.

But he heard her and his throat tightened.

Then Janice said, "Do you see what you've done, Daniel?"

"I haven't done anything. Put the gun down and let's talk about this." Mason had to give the man credit. He kept his voice low, his anger tempered.

"There's nothing to talk about. This is all your fault. Now tell them to go away and leave me alone. You're the big bad detective always bragging about your connections and power in the department. Now would be a good time to put it to use."

Mason heard a muffled sigh. "Janice, this is beyond the scope of my power. Please, just put the gun down and come out. No one has died yet. No one has to." A pause. "Your father will get you out of this with just a slap on the wrist."

Mason saw Bethany's eyes narrow and her no
trils flare. He raised a finger to his lips and sh
clamped her mouth shut. But he could see sh
wanted desperately to say something.

She didn't understand that Daniel was tellin
Janice anything she wanted to hear. Anything th
might get her to drop that gun from Bethany'
head.

"Daddy." Janice snorted. "Daddy always hate
you. I never understood why. But now I do. Yc
weren't good enough for me. Just a cop wh
thought he was a big man…."

As Janice ranted her ire, her attention slippe
from Bethany. But her finger tightened on th
trigger.

And Lacey acted a nanosecond before Maso
was going to move. She dove at the woman ju
as a gunshot sounded.

As though in slow motion, Mason watched
happen. Lacey's outstretched arms rammed int
Janice's midsection. The air whooshed from he
and the two women fell to the floor. Anothe
gunshot.

Mason grabbed Bethany and passed her to
fellow officer who hustled her from the room.

"Mom! Mom!" The girl's screams echoe
behind her.

Neither Lacey nor Janice moved and Mason fe
like his heart might stop. "Lacey!"

Ignoring the chaos around him, he bolted to her side and pulled her from on top of Janice.

Crimson stared back at him.

"Oh no. Oh no, please, God, no," he whispered.

"Is she hurt?" Catelyn knelt beside him.

"I don't know." Frantically, he placed his fingers against the side of her neck. Relief filled him. "I've got a pulse." But where was all the blood coming from?

Catelyn looked at him. "Janice is dead."

"We need paramedics here now!" Mason hollered.

"They're on the way," Joseph said from behind him.

Heart pounding in his throat, Mason found the wound. Some of the blood was Lacey's. She'd been shot in the side. He placed his hand over the area and pressed.

He looked up, hoping to find help on the way, only to see Daniel in the doorway, gun lowered to his side. Who did he shoot?

Before he could voice the question, EMTs rushed in. Mason moved out of the way and watched intently while they worked on Lacey. *Please, don't let her die.* The prayer slipped from him and he realized he meant it, believed God heard it.

But would He answer it the way Mason wanted?

Soon, efficient hands fitted Lacey with an oxygen mask and lifted her onto the stretcher. She moaned and rolled her head, her eyes flickering for a brief moment. Mason's throat tightened. "Is she going to be okay?"

The younger EMT looked at him. "Her vitals are good. She's breathing well, so it doesn't look like the bullet hit anything vital like a lung, however, that's up to a doctor to determine."

Mason felt slightly better. "I'm right behind you." And he would be as soon as he introduced himself to his daughter.

Watching Lacey roll away was one of the hardest things he'd ever done, everything in him wanting to be with her, but he knew she'd want him to take care of Bethany.

In the care of two officers, Bethany didn't see him approach until he was standing in front of her. She looked up and went still.

They eyed each other for a long minute then her lower lip quivered and her eyes filled with tears once again. She stood and stepped toward him. Then hesitated.

His heart clenching, he held out his arms.

With a muffled cry, she threw herself into them, resting her head against his chest. She was slightly taller than Lacey and he lay his cheek against her hair for a brief moment. "Your mom's on her way to the hospital."

"She was shot, wasn't she?"

"Yes." His stomach churned at the thought.

A sob hiccupped through her and her arms tightened around his waist. Then she pulled back and palmed her eyes like a two-year-old. "Is she gonna be okay?"

"I think so, but I'm going to the hospital to meet her and they're going to want to check you out, too." An ambulance and two EMTs waited to transport her. "You want me to ride with you?"

"Yeah." A brief pause. "Are you my dad?"

He nodded and his eyes misted.

She sighed and said, "Good. I'm glad."

Mason gave a little laugh. "Me, too, Bethany."

"I'm sorry for all the trouble I caused," she whispered.

"You didn't cause any trouble. That was all Janice."

"Who is she?"

"A woman who used to be your mother's best friend growing up." He shook his head. "A woman with some serious mental-health issues brought on by a lot of things."

He watched a tremor wrack the girl. "I thought she was trying to help me. I told the police that someone came up behind me while I was on the phone with you and stabbed me with something.

Almost immediately, I started feeling all woozy
I couldn't stand up or—" She broke off and shud
dered again.

Mason nodded toward the ambulance. He wa
ready to check on Lacey. From the corner of hi
eye, he saw Catelyn nod to him. He gave her
thumbs-up and climbed into the back of the ambu
lance with Bethany.

The EMT shot him a look and he saw the pro
test forming on the man's lips. Mason flashe
his badge and the EMT paused, shrugged an
reached around him to shut the door. Bethan
climbed onto the gurney and sat there while th
EMT checked her vitals once more.

"I'm fine," she assured them.

"It's standard procedure, Bethany. Just let hin
check you over, all right?"

She lifted a shoulder and nodded. "Fine."

His heart fluttered. How many times had h
made that same gesture with that same shoulder
While she was occupied, he drank in her feature
noting the light reddish-blond hair, the blue eye
that matched his, the shape of her jaw.

He was in awe. And a deep sadness stole ove
him at what he'd missed. But a rock-hard deter
mination soon replaced it. He vowed to make u
for lost time. He wouldn't live another day withou
being a part of Bethany's life.

His phone sounded, jerking him out of hi

usings and he grabbed it in the middle of the second ring. "Hello?"

"Hey, this is Catelyn. Just wanted to let you now we found a name on a slip of paper in Janice's purse. Billy Rose."

The name set off bells in his mind, but he ouldn't place it. "Who's that?"

"One of the more seedy shelter residents Janice ribed into keeping an eye out for Bethany. When e heard he was going to be charged with attempted murder, he had a lot to talk about."

"So he's the one that injected her. So Daniel idn't lie about that."

"Yep. He saw her at the phone booth, grabbed he drug Janice had supplied him with sometime arlier and went after Bethany. We found five hundred dollars in an old coat pocket he had stuffed p under his bunk."

"That must have seemed like a fortune to him." Mason blew out a sigh and said, "All right. Thanks or keeping me updated."

He hung up and passed the information on to Bethany who bit her lip. "I don't care about him. want to know how my mom's doing."

So did he.

He dialed the hospital number from memory. He'd spent so much time there, he'd had no choice but to memorize the number.

Lacey, no doubt, had been taken in through

Emergency. After being connected to several dif
ferent sources, he finally landed on the right one.
"Lacey Gibson." Impatience ate at him, but he
kept his cool. "She was brought in with a gunsho
wound probably about twenty minutes ago."

"She's in surgery right now. That's all the infor
mation I have."

It was enough for now. "Thanks."

He hung up and told Bethany, "She's in
surgery."

Her eyes closed for a brief moment. "She saved
my life."

"I know."

"That woman was going to kill me."

"Yeah, she was." He had no doubt, Janice had
no intention of letting Bethany out of there alive.
She'd been determined to make Lacey pay for
having a child when hers had died. "Don't dwell
on that, okay? Think about all the good times
we're going to have catching up on fifteen missing
years."

"I'm kinda mad at her," Bethany voiced in a
low tone.

"Well, to be honest, I am, too, but I've gotten
to know your mom all over again in the last few
days and she made the decisions she made, and
she had some valid reasons for doing so." He took
her hand and looked into her eyes. "We can hold

n to our anger and have a lot of miserable years head of us or we can let it go and start over."

Bethany went quiet and just stared at him. Then slow smile started at the corners of her lips and pread until her pale face glowed. "You still love er, don't you?"

Mason felt the flush start at the base of his neck. Clearing his throat, he said, "Well…ah…"

"Don't you?"

"Yeah. I do." There, he'd admitted it.

Bethany squealed and Mason got a brief glimpse f what she might have been like as a toddler. He herished that moment.

The EMT had done what he needed to do with Bethany and at this point just sat back and let them alk.

Mason appreciated it. And as much as he wanted to spend time with Bethany, he couldn't eep his thoughts from Lacey. Anxious to get to he hospital to check on her, he rubbed his palms n his jeans-clad thighs and blew out a sigh.

After what seemed like an eternity, the ambu-ance pulled up to the hospital's Emergency ntrance.

Mason hopped out the back and turned to Beth-ny. "Go get checked out. Give me a chance to ind out something about your mom and I'll come ind you, okay?"

"No! I want to go with you. I'm fine!"

She got up from the gurney, shoving off th
hands that attempted to restrain her.

"Bethany, you really…" He clamped his mout
shut. The set of her jaw—the one that was ju
like his—said he could talk until judgment da
but he wasn't going to change her mind. She wa
going with him one way or another. He looked a
the EMT. "We'll be fine. Thanks."

"I just need a signature."

Mason scribbled his name on the form, too
Bethany's hand and went to find Lacey.

TWENTY-ONE

What truck did I step out in front of? Lacey wondered as pain shot along her left side. She moved, blinked and saw a figure standing beside her.

Vaguely she registered that the figure was calling her name, telling her to wake up.

"Don't want to," she muttered. Or thought she did. Her tongue felt funny.

Water. She desperately wanted something to drink.

Something cool and wet pressed against her lips and she swallowed, feeling the slight amount of water soothe her throat.

She wanted more.

She blinked again and felt the rest of her senses kick in. She sniffed. A hospital.

Her fingers twitched and moved, feeling the sheet. And a bed. She was in a hospital bed. Why?

"Mom? Come on, Mom, time to wake up."

Bethany called her. She had to wake up, her daughter needed her.

That last thought was enough to force her eye lids up and open.

And there stood Bethany.

It all came back to her in a terrifying rush.

"Bethany," she whispered.

"Hey, Mom."

"You're okay." Something wet splashed on her hand. "Don't cry, Bethany, I'll be fine."

"Umm, that wasn't me."

With a start, Lacey realized the water had come from the other side. She rolled her head on the pillow to come face-to-face with Mason.

His hands gripped hers and he gave her fingers a gentle squeeze. He blinked and she saw the moisture there.

"Hey," she whispered.

"Hey."

Bethany stood. "I'm going to go down to the cafeteria and tell Grandma and Grandpa you're okay."

Her daughter leaned over and gave her a gentle hug, avoiding contact with her left side. Lacey snagged her hand. "You're really here? You're all right?"

"Yeah, Mom, I'm fine."

"Okay."

Bethany exited the room leaving her alone with the man she'd never fallen out of love with.

He looked haggard, worn out. And oh, so good.

"I almost lost you again," he stated in a hoarse voice.

"Aw, I wasn't going anywhere," she tried to joke.

It fell flat.

"You almost got yourself killed."

"But Bethany's fine, so it's all good." She grimaced. "Who shot me?"

He sighed. "Janice's gun went off when you tackled her, so technically Janice did."

"What happened to Janice?"

"Daniel shot her. She died at the scene."

Lacey gasped, then winced at the pain in her side. Tears welled for her old friend, for the girl she grew up with, not the woman she'd become. "I'm so sorry."

"She let anger and bitterness rule her heart for so long that eventually there wasn't room for anything else. I'm not going to let that happen to us again." He leaned forward and placed a kiss on her forehead. "I love you, Lacey," he whispered. "I always have. I was a fool to believe Daniel over you."

Emotion clogged her throat. How she'd longed to hear those words from him. "I love you,

Mason, I really do. Can you forgive me for keeping Bethany from you? For making you miss the first fifteen years of her life?"

"I already have. Can you forgive me for being an immature jerk who wouldn't listen?"

"Yeah." She blinked at another onslaught of tears. "I can do that."

Mason leaned down and placed a kiss on her lips. "As soon as you're better, will you marry me?"

She couldn't stop the tears from flowing. "I'll have to ask Bethany, but if she says it's okay, then I would love to."

"Bethany says yes."

Mason and Lacey jerked their gaze to the girl who stood in the doorway with a sheepish look on her face. "Sorry. I was coming back to get my purse and couldn't help but overhear." She gestured to the small bag and Lacey shook her head.

"How in the world did you manage to hold on to that thing all this time?"

A serious expression crossed Bethany's face as she walked over to pick up the purse. She opened it and pulled out a picture. Turning it around, she showed it Lacey. Stunned, Lacey realized it a picture of the two of them taken at the beach two years ago.

"Because the only way I could stay strong was

look at this and remember why I was running. Why I had to stay away from you." Tears started to drip down her cheeks, and Mason grabbed a tissue from the box by the bed.

He handed it to her then offered her a hug. "You did good, Bethany. You did real good, okay?"

"Yeah," she whispered. She stepped back from his embrace and in a more chipper voice, asked, "So, what's my role in this whole wedding thing?"

Mason took her hand and smiled down at her. "Daughter of the groom."

Lacey motioned them next to her, then moved closer and she took Bethany's other hand. "And daughter of the bride."

"The missing piece of the puzzle?"

"No way," Mason said. "The last piece of the puzzle. The piece that makes the picture complete."

She grinned at her parents. "I like that."

They all did.

* * * * *

Dear Reader,

I hope you enjoyed Mason and Lacey's story.
sure had a good time writing it. When I first ha
the glimmer of the idea for the story, I didn't pla
on it being a prodigal story—a story of a child tha
was lost but was found and finally made her wa
home. However, that's what happened. Althoug
it took Lacey's father a little time to come aroun
Lacey's mother welcomed her and Bethany hom
with wide-open arms. I pray that if you've drifte
from the Lord that you will run home to Him an
be swept up into those heavenly arms that hol
you close and *always* welcome you home. I woul
love to hear what you think about this story. Fee
free to email me at: lynetteeason@lynetteeaso
com. And if you have time, please feel free t
stop by my website to sign up for my newslette
at www.lynetteeason.com.

God Bless!
Until we meet again,

Lynette Eason

QUESTIONS FOR DISCUSSION

1. When Lacey realized she had to act fast in order to find Bethany, she was willing to put aside her feelings and go to the one person she felt could help her. Have you ever had to put aside feelings to do something you knew you were supposed to do?

2. Mason is shocked when Lacey appears on his doorstep. He's even more shocked when she makes the life-changing announcement that he's a father. How have you reacted to life-changing news—whether good or bad?

3. Mason's pride and hurt caused him to miss out on the first fifteen years of his daughter's life. That may seem extreme, but pride has caused a lot of problems for people over the years. Has it ever caused you a problem? If so, what? Did you resolve it?

4. Mason has placed God on the back burner of his life, so to speak. Up to the point that Lacey enters his life again, he hasn't really seen a need for God. Where is your

relationship with God? Do you have a need for Him?

5. Lacey grew up in a Christian home. At least she was in church every Sunday and learned right from wrong. What are your impressions of Lacey's parents and their reactions toward her when she found herself pregnant?

6. Some people may think sending a pregnant daughter off to a home for unwed mothers old-fashioned or an ancient way of thinking. Actually, there are some very good homes around the country that do the things Lacey described, when she was telling Mason about her experiences there. What do you think about this idea?

7. What do you think about the idea of sending a pregnant teenager away to have her baby? In Lacey's case, she realized it was the best thing that could have happened to her. Do you agree?

8. What if Lacey were your daughter? What would you do? Or what *did* you do if you've experienced this situation?

9. What was your favorite scene in the book and why?

0. What kind of mother do you think Lacey is?

1. Did you understand Lacey's anger and bitterness toward her parents? Toward Mason?

2. Did you think it took Lacey too long to come home after she accepted Christ and turned her life around?

3. Did you understand Lacey's fears of telling Bethany about Mason? Was her fear (based on her last experience with Mason) that Mason would reject Bethany realistic?

4. Bethany said she felt like a lost or missing puzzle piece and that she was still searching for where she fit in (her puzzle). Have you ever felt like that? Have you found your puzzle (the place where you fit in)?

5. Mason was a Christian at the beginning of the story, but his faith was kind of on the back burner. Life had been going pretty well

for him in his career, etc. But then he find
out he has a daughter. A daughter in dange
How did that bring him back to the God h
once loved?

LARGER-PRINT BOOKS!

GET 2 FREE LARGER-PRINT NOVELS PLUS 2 FREE MYSTERY GIFTS

Love Inspired

SUSPENSE

RIVETING INSPIRATIONAL ROMANCE

Larger-print novels are now available...

YES! Please send me 2 FREE LARGER-PRINT Love Inspired® Suspense novels and my 2 FREE mystery gifts (gifts are worth about $10). After receiving them, if I don't wish to receive any more books, I can return the shipping statement marked "cancel". If I don't cancel, I will receive 4 brand-new novels every month and be billed just $4.74 per book in the U.S. or $5.24 per book in Canada. That's a saving of over 20% off the cover price. It's quite a bargain! Shipping and handling is just 50¢ per book.* I understand that accepting the 2 free books and gifts places me under no obligation to buy anything. I can always return a shipment and cancel at any time. Even if I never buy another book, the two free books and gifts are mine to keep forever.

110/310 IDN E7RD

Name	(PLEASE PRINT)	
Address		Apt. #
City	State/Prov.	Zip/Postal Code

Signature (if under 18, a parent or guardian must sign)

Mail to **Steeple Hill Reader Service:**
IN U.S.A.: P.O. Box 1867, Buffalo, NY 14240-1867
IN CANADA: P.O. Box 609, Fort Erie, Ontario L2A 5X3

Not valid for current subscribers to Love Inspired Suspense larger-print books.

**Are you a current subscriber to Love Inspired Suspense books and want to receive the larger-print edition?
Call 1-800-873-8635 or visit www.morefreebooks.com.**

* Terms and prices subject to change without notice. Prices do not include applicable taxes. Sales tax applicable in N.Y. Canadian residents will be charged applicable provincial taxes and GST. Offer not valid in Quebec. This offer is limited to one order per household. All orders subject to approval. Credit or debit balances in a customer's account(s) may be offset by any other outstanding balance owed by or to the customer. Please allow 4 to 6 weeks for delivery. Offer available while quantities last.

Your Privacy: Steeple Hill Books is committed to protecting your privacy. Our Privacy Policy is available online at www.SteepleHill.com or upon request from the Reader Service. From time to time we make our lists of customers available to reputable third parties who may have a product or service of interest to you. If you would prefer we not share your name and address, please check here. ☐

Help us get it right—We strive for accurate, respectful and relevant communications. To clarify or modify your communication preferences, visit us at www.ReaderService.com/consumerchoice.

LISUSLP10R